BIGFOOT
TERROR IN THE WOODS
Sightings and Encounters / vol. 3

by William J. Sheehan

Whether or not Bigfoot is real or imagined is something that is yet to be determined. Therefore this book is a work of fiction. Names, characters, locations and incidents are either the results of the interviewees imaginations, or if they are true, have not been proven to be so. Any resemblance to actual people be they living or dead, or any events of any kind is purely coincidental in nature.

If you've seen something, say something.

Email splinters@optonline.net

For media inquiries contact splinters@optonline.net

Cover and text design by Casey Smith, hello@sugarstudiosdesign.com

Contents

The Grizzly Encounter

This account was brought to my attention by Sam Longfooter, who just happens to be an American Indian. I joked with Sam on our interview about someone with his last name having the encounter which you shall soon read. Here is what Mr. Longfooter had to say:

In 2008, we were going up into the Tongass National Forest region for a grizzly bear hunt, Alaskan style. Having flown into Ketchikan, we had arranged for a guide service to meet up with us. He had a thirty-six foot trawler-style ship with a twenty foot aluminum tender in tow; the plan being to get us in close proximity via the Behm Canal to where we would hunt. Thereafter, we would anchor the trawler and take the skiff up into the Unuk River to establish our camp and begin the hunt.

I am not going to lie to you. You can easily die on a grizzly hunt and many have through the years. You can do everything right and have your gun jam at the critical moment in which you are firing your shot and be mauled to death. I always hunt grizzly with one or two armed men, besides myself, for this reason. And yes, the gun jamming has actually happened to me personally, with a grizzly charging at us from seventy feet away. If my guide had not been at the ready, I would not be here with you today.

My guide for this hunt was a well-seasoned, old timer who knew this area well. When it came to grizzlies, he was renowned for his ability to consistently score the largest of the large. The plan was to take the tender into the zone each day from the main ship and hunt the woods, returning to the main ship every afternoon to eat and sleep until we found our mark.

The forest by the river is perpetually damp and shadowy. Its floor is covered predominantly in a layer of thick, spongy, green moss which silences not only our steps, but those of the bear as well. This, at times, makes one ask the question: just who is stalking who? For if you are not careful, the tables can be swiftly turned, leaving you wishing that you had never been born.

On our first day in, we had come across numerous tracks that were fresh and large. We also had located numerous tree scrapes, indicating a large bear was in the area. That afternoon, it started to rain and rain hard. I had learned many years ago to leave the woods if it started to rain while hunting bear. Sound is such a critical aspect that, to have it drowned out by a noisy rainfall, can prove to be deadly. And so it was that we left the woods for the remainder of the day. Unfortunately, it kept raining throughout the night, as well as into the following day. So we had made the decision, as a group, to stay put in the ship until the weather became more favorable.

On the third day, we were back in the woods. The forest was

soaked. As we walked, our boots were sinking into the moss three to four inches with every step that we took. The bear's prints which we had seen the other day were quite large, indicating that a seriously big bear was on the prowl. At times in here, we couldn't see, with clarity, more than thirty feet ahead or to the side of us. Knowing that a large grizzly could cover ground quickly, we were all on edge.

We were making our way in deep when we ran across a second set of prints that were not from a bear. Immediately, we all knew what they were from. These prints were well over twenty-four inches long and ten inches wide. Some of them were at least a foot deep or more into the moss. We were now following the tracks of a bear and a Sasquatch. This was quite a duo to be in the woods with, and not being able to hear nor see them could prove to be devastating. We had been tracking what we believed to be a thousand pound bear, based on the size of its tracks. And now, based on the size of the Sasquatch tracks, God only knows what this thing would weigh in at. I was not ignorant of the beast and neither was my guide. This was an extremely dicey and dangerous situation, but curiosity had gotten the best of us. We moved forward.

There were hundreds and hundreds of tracks laid down in line with each other, moving off in the direction we were now heading. It was then that the realization came upon me that we were no longer interested in the grizzly. We were now stalking a Sasquatch through this dense and treacherous forest. It must have been about an hour into our hike with the trail having not gone cold in the least. We started to break out of the damp forest into a clearing, filled with tall grass and clusters of trees. This was the absolute worst case scenario imaginable for stalking a bear or anything else. A grizzly could come busting out of here at any moment and be on us before we knew what happened. We weren't making a sound as we walked, like we were walking on a mattress with bare feet. It was almost instantaneous that, as we entered this field, a stench of what I can only describe as being raw, fresh shit, hit all of our nostrils at the same time. It was the foulest smelling odor that you could imagine and it was overwhelming us almost to the point of gagging.

As we stood there, some areas of the grass and brush ahead of us appeared to be some six feet tall or better. While we were coming to grips with the stench and what was before us, a huge figure started to rise up out of the grass some fifty feet from where we stood. As soon as we saw it, we knew what it was. We ducked down in unison. Although we were hidden, the problem now was that we couldn't see what we knew was the Sasquatch. If he should decide to turn and retrace his steps, it would surely be a gunfight.

As we sat, squatting, we could hear some grunting sounds coming from the beast. Then, everything went quiet. We wouldn't dare stand up and remained squatting with our guns pointed straight ahead for some thirty minutes or more; expecting that, at any moment, the grass in front of us would part, revealing this hideous monster. I was the first one who actually stood to my feet to have a look-see. It was safe, and I waved for the guide to back out of where we were. We made it all the way back to the tender and then to the ship, having made the decision to quit the hunt for the day. To a man, we believed that this Sasquatch was squatting in the brush, relieving itself, and had just stood up, with its back to us, as we ducked down.

The following day, we were not prepared to give up on this location, knowing that a huge grizzly was on the prowl. We put the gear into the skiff and, once again, went ashore. We began to scout out the forest in the same way we had the day before, but were not coming across any new grizzly tracks, other than the ones from the previous day's hunt.

In similar fashion to the day before, about an hour into the hunt, we once again came upon a new set of Sasquatch prints; only this time, there were two sets of tracks paralleling each other. There were many of them, with one set being much larger than the other. Our hunch, at the time, was that the grizzly had moved out, either because of the competition or, perhaps, because it wasn't willing to put up a territorial fight for its domain. This was all a guess because we really don't know anything about the relationships between these creatures, but the facts being what they were, the bear was gone and now there were two Sasquatch in the area.

The day before, as the Sasquatch began to stand, we squatted down immediately upon seeing him. Having said as much, I still saw that its body, not yet standing fully erect, was at least four feet taller than the surrounding grass. I am six feet tall and some of the grass was taller than me. We knew that this larger Sasquatch was, at the very least, all of eleven to twelve feet tall. Additionally, we already knew the size of its feet, having tracked it through the forest and into the field. We had decided, yet again, to track these two sets as far as we could without getting into a compromised position as we had the day before.

It must have been at least a mile or more into the stalk when we came upon a large decaying tree on the ground, covered in moss. The tree, for the most part, in the center of its remaining trunk, had been freshly torn apart. Both sets of prints were present, overlapping each other around the entire trunk. We now knew that these Sasquatch were, more than likely, harvesting grubs from the decaying tree. It's funny, but this is the type of thing which is actually taught in survivalist training. Grubs can serve as a source of food for humans who find themselves in dire straits. Unwilling to carry on the search any further, having come for a grizzly and not a Sasquatch, we aborted the hunt and went back to the ship.

Two days later, I had scored a large bear several miles away on the northwest side of the river. No further evidence of Sasquatch was seen or heard. I cannot emphasize enough the fear that came upon me when I was suddenly confronted with the enormity of this monster standing up in front of us that day. The sheer size and dimensions of what we could see were staggering. Even with my rifle in hand, I felt it wouldn't be enough if it had charged. By the time a bullet would have done it in, we would have been dead for sure. You just can't believe it and yet, there it is standing before you.

From the waist up and looking at the back, which was our perspective, I was looking at what appeared to be the shape of an old-fashioned kite. The middle of the longer, bottom section of the kite being its waist, which was more than likely three or more feet wide. The back, angling up even wider to the area of the shoulders, would be seen as the main rib area of the kite. The shoulders were probably something along the lines of seven feet wide. The upper, angled section of the kite would be its upper trapezius muscles. These muscles were so large, that they were obscuring almost its entire head from view. I believe I was only looking at maybe 1/3 of its head because of the immense size of its muscles.

It's Not Wood

This unusual and rather game changing story was told to me by Frank Micelli, a landscape photographer and avid hiker from the Pacific Northwest. Here is what Frank saw and heard when hiking through Lower Crabtree Meadows in July of 2017:

As I told you when we first spoke, I am more or less an amateur photographer, specializing in landscape and panoramic pictures. I don't know when or how someone is touted to be a professional in my craft, but I have never applied that badge to myself. I have been at this now for well over twenty-five years, and many of my pictures are posted online at sites, such as Flikr.

My wife, Sandra, and I were just coming off some high ground, working our way down and through Lower Crab Meadows. I had just set the tripod up with the view of the valley and trees within the Meadows in the foreground and with Mount Russell rising up in the background. Having taken a few really nice shots from this perspective, the two of us continued to hike through the Crab, as we call it. As we made our way through, we had decided to work our way up to a slightly higher position on one of the wooded hilltops to our left side. We had hiked up through the trees to a slightly higher elevation where the perspective through the lens had changed dramatically. Once again, I had set up the tripod to take a few more shots. The view from here was spectacular. I was standing alongside of the camera setting up for a panoramic shot when a loud knocking sound emanated through this valley.

Sandra and I both looked at each other as if to say, *what the heck was that?* We began to scan the surrounding area in hopes of seeing whatever had made the sound. I should mention that we hadn't seen any large animals as we passed through the Crab getting to the point where we found ourselves. I was using the telephoto camera lens and Sandra was using a pair of field glasses to scan the area around us. After a few minutes, having heard nothing more, my wife said she saw something dark pacing around in the timber on the slope to our right hand side. I said to her, "What do you mean *pacing*?"

She said to me that, whatever she was looking at, was standing on two legs and was moving back and forth in a random manner within the trees. I immediately started scanning the area in which she was looking with my telephoto and bingo!

There, before my eyes, was a large, black Bigfoot on the slope. Just so you can visualize what I was seeing through the lens, the creature was about two inches tall in the lens at this distance. I had it in focus, but I couldn't see it or its movements with great clarity. It was pacing around, exactly as my wife had said; flipping its arms left and right, like a nervous man waiting for a late bus.

It stayed in this one small area, pacing around for maybe ten minutes or so.

Suddenly, it stopped pacing and stood erect, facing the north with its head held high, and brought its hands up to its mouth. We once again heard a loud, resonating knock. As soon as we had heard the knocking sound, it lowered its arms and started pacing around, as it had been doing before.

Now, I must be upfront with you with what I am about to say. My wife and I had seen every Bigfoot show available to mankind ten times over. We had heard all of the tales and seen all of the people pounding on trees with logs and bats walking through the forest. The two of us, in all of our outdoor adventures, have seen and heard nothing for ourselves up until this afternoon of which I speak. On that afternoon, I believe we settled the score once and for all, as far as wood knocks go. It is not a wood knock at all, but rather a large and loud vocalization being made by the creatures internally. Having tried it for myself, I can make a cluck or knock sound by putting my tongue to the roof of my mouth and moving my jaw downward. There is no way for me to describe the mechanics of what I am talking about to you, but I can do it. Now, whether or not they are doing it in the same way is something which you and I have no way of knowing, but what I saw and heard was evidence enough for me. There was nothing else present in that valley with us, and the sound occurred exactly when it had elevated its head and put its hands to the sides of its mouth.

The creature was evidently very tall and broad in stature. Exactly how big, I cannot say, because the distance was far too great and we weren't going over there to say hello. We could most definitely make out the exceedingly long arm length and its fur, or hair, was shiny and black. After about what must have been twenty or so minutes, it abruptly stopped this pacing and moved out of our sight; walking what I would say was some three or four hundred yards.

I, as a photographer, have captured some moments in time that will never be duplicated again. I have shown the same stills to many others that you have seen and they frankly don't believe it or have little or nothing to say about them. I guess it's just part of human nature. We have the believers and the non-believers. We have those who do and those who don't. As for Sandra and myself, we are most definitely now counted among the believers.

The Grey Whale Sighting

This rather unusual sighting and evidentiary finding was brought to me by Henry Lakewood and his friend, Lyle Mitchum; both of them being residents of Washington State. Here is what they saw and found while doing a little beachcombing:

It was in June of 2011, that Lyle and I were stretching our legs on the shoreline, about twenty miles south of Cape Flattery and maybe, ten miles due east of the Olympic National Park. You can get very close to the shore here via the highway and we were hiking below a short bluff, which is inclusive of a protected narrow band of wildlife management zone. The time of day was about 7:30 a.m. when we began our hike. There is a large stretch of shoreline, consisting of many miles, which Lyle and I regularly hike at different points and times of the year. Lyle is an artist and comes here to collect drift-wood to use in sculptures.

We were hugging the bluff, scavenging through the debris from the high tide looking for some good finds, when we were just approaching a bend in the bluff to our left. Once around this bend, a long stretch of beach comes into view, which extends for many miles to the south. As soon as our eyes were clear of the bluff, we could see two large, darkly colored figures moving around a large mass laying on the shore. One of the figures was standing and the other appeared to be down on the ground, moving around. From the distance, it looked like it may have been two men wearing coveralls or foul weather gear, so we continued heading in their direction. I don't think we walked another hundred feet when the guy on the ground stood up and the man who was standing turned around quickly to look in our direction. No sooner had this happened than the two of them took off, scurrying up the side of the bluff and out of sight.

This whole thing was very bizarre as it unfolded. As weird as this all may sound to you, picture us walking down this lonely stretch of shore and having this occur before our own eyes. We continued to walk down to where they had been. As we got closer, we could now see that the mass on the beach was, in fact, a dead juvenile grey whale. The whale was obviously dead and had an enormous wound on its side. To us, it appeared to be the result of what may have been a great white or, perhaps, a killer whale attack. It appeared to have died and washed up on the beach before being eaten. I now realized, standing over the whale, that what I was seeing from the distance was one guy holding up the upper jaw of the whale and the other guy was on the ground doing something within the mouth area of the whale. There was a lot of meat, for lack of a better word, and debris laying around the mouth of this whale on the beach. It seemed as though they had been going through the mouth to harvest the interior of the whale.

As we stood there, taking this all in and trying to make some sense of it, our eyes now turned to the bluff where the figures had exited. It was fairly tall and steep, and we could see where they had climbed up it. We looked it over and determined that neither of us thought we could scale it at all, let alone at a fast pace. These two guys had made it up it in seconds.

Moving closer to the bluff's base, our eyes were opened to what we had been seeing. There were several, very large and well-made, bare footprints at the base of the bluff. They were similar to a human's, but extremely large and broad in nature. The two of us, not being ignorant, now realized we had just seen two Bigfoot scavenging a whale carcass and making a hasty exit up the bluff. With the Olympic National Park and Forest being in reasonably close proximity to our location, and the fact of the matter being that there is nothing around here to speak of to begin with, we now knew that they were in the area. The picture had now come together as to what we were seeing. I know, speaking for myself, that I was thinking, *what the heck are two guys doing out here in black fishermen's raingear?* And even if they were coveralls, they would be inappropriate for the day's conditions, which were very mild. I did notice that, as they started to run, their movements looked very strange. Their steps and arm swings looked disproportionate in comparison to what we are used to seeing from a human perspective. Now we knew the reason why: we had just seen two Bigfoot on the shore.

Well, my dear readers, it doesn't surprise me at all that Bigfoot are so well adapted at taking advantage of any and all food sources as they become available to them. Fresh food is fresh food, wherever, and whoever, you are.

The Bone Pile

This unusual story came to me by way of Terry Wade, a resident of the state of Washington. Let's listen in as we hear what Terry had to say:

As I thought about having this discussion with you today, I felt it would be best to lay a little ground work as to who I am and what I do. It may help to add credence to what I am about to say to both you and your readers. First of all, I am a third generation grocer and now, food wholesaler. This business, which I now run and own, was started as a grocery store in New York in 1905. Today, having taken over the business many years ago from my father, we are strictly a wholesale vegetable distributor to the restaurant and food service industry, predominantly in New York, Connecticut, and New Jersey. I have a great managerial and employee base that affords me a surplus of free time, with me being able to accomplish most of what I have to do via phone and internet.

Since I don't really need to be there, except for the occasional fly in, I have lived in numerous locations throughout the country over the past twenty years or so. I am currently in Washington. In preparation to talk with you, I was trying to settle on a number in my mind as to how many days I have spent in the woods hunting. To the best of my knowledge, I came up with somewhere between 1,200 and 1,500 days on the hunt. This would be inclusive of both small and large game, including waterfowl and eight safaris. I am reasonably proficient in the disciplines of rifle, shotgun and bow and consider myself at this point in the game, a decent tracker as well. I have seen a Bigfoot, but that's not why I really called you. I called about some evidence that I had found, and a little experiment that I did, in hopes of furthering the cause of Bigfoot being real. It's not that I need anyone to convince me, you understand…

In the fall of 2006, while stalking some deer in the fringes of the Pasayten Wilderness, I had a large Bigfoot pass above my position on a hillside while I was on the hunt below. As I said, I am not here to speak of this sighting because I frankly don't have much to say about it. I saw it, it was real, and that's it. What I do want to talk about is the subsequent bone pile that I came across and my experimentation regarding it.

In 2008, I was stalking in the area of the Henry M. Jackson Wilderness, west of Chelan, when I came into an area that was devoid of, shall I say, all warm blooded animals. It must have been for well over a mile before I realized that there was absolutely no creatures, be they great or small, to be found in this area; a fact that was extremely unusual in and of itself. A short time later, I came upon what I will describe as a small clearing which was scattered with the bones of just about everything that lives in these parts. I am talking from skulls to legs and everything in between. Now it's not that I stood there counting or anything like that, but there were so many bones from so many different animals that it would be impossible to determine what belonged to what. Just so you understand, if you were to shoot a deer in the woods and leave it be, in six months' time, there would be zero trace of the animal's body left. In fact, it is my opinion that the skull is the last to go because that is, virtually, the only thing I ever find when hunting. Perhaps there is less marrow in the skull, but other than that, I really don't know why.

Regardless, the fact that all of these bones were here and that there was no wildlife around really got my attention. I decided to do some experiments in the area over the next year or so. It was some three months later that I came into this area again and took down a deer about two miles away from this bone pile. Now what I did was not right as it pertains to hunting, but this was an experiment and for just this one time I broke all the rules. I shot the deer and left it in the woods so that I could come back to it over time and log what happened to its carcass. I had seen a show about a place called The Body Farm, many years ago. This was an outdoor forensics laboratory where human donor bodies were allowed to remain, in various states, outside in order to determine the rates of decomposition under a variety of circumstances. This study would then better enable law enforcement to determine the time of death for bodies found buried, laying in the woods, or even in the trunks of cars, for that matter.

As far as the deer was concerned, and my inability to come in here every day, I had determined that somewhere between four and six months was needed for this deer to vanish without so much as a trace. There was absolutely nothing left and this had happened less than two miles away from the bone pile, which was still there and untouched. I must also mention that any hunter worth their salt will tell you that no predatory animal, be they bear, lion, wolf, fox, coyote or anything else, will take their kill back to the same location over and over again. Whatever they don't eat will be eaten by something else fairly quickly. Having done my little experiment only two miles from the sight of the bone pile, I went back and set up three game cameras, in low and high positions, near the pile and left them for a month.

When I went back in and retrieved the cameras, not so much as one picture had been taken. I reset the area and came back a month later, finding two of the cameras missing and one smashed on the ground. It looked like it was hit from the front side with what I will describe as a punch. I say this because there was no damage, such as a rock or a log would have done, to the plastic that was visible to my eyes. I took the camera home and disassembled it on my work bench in hopes of salvaging the card. Thankfully, the card was unaffected by the assault. When I reviewed the card, there were two pictures. In the first image, I saw what appeared to be the dark fingers of a hand that must have come from the side into view, but it was very fuzzy. The second image was completely dark, as though the lens was facing or being held against something dark in color, and that was it.

After having performed my experiments, my own personal conviction is this: the bone pile is a place where a Bigfoot is returning to, over and over again, to eat. For what reason, I do not know. Secondly, the animals in the area surrounding this place will have nothing to do with what this creature had touched; steering clear of the entire area for quite some distance. Again, the reason for this being a mystery, at this time. It's also rather remarkable that as I came in to the area the first time, it was at about a mile away that all life was seemingly gone in the woods. And yet, at two miles' distance, my deer had been completely consumed. This made it clear to me that the Bigfoot's saliva on these bones, or something about it, had created a large barrier of some sort around its kill. At least one thing is now clear in my own mind: nothing in the forest wants anything to do with Bigfoot. Within any other species, animals will contend for another's kill. If nothing else, they will return to get their fill of what another may have left behind.

The Red Buttes Beast

The following sighting was described to me by Mitchell Langley, a resident of California. Here is what Mitchell saw while hiking with his wife:

My wife, Edna, and I had started our hike from the Seiad Valley and were working our way up north into the Rogue River- Siskiyou National Forest; our destination being the Red Buttes Wilderness area. Edna and I had been through this area many times and knew it probably as well as anyone on the planet. We had started early and made our way into what we refer to as The Red Zone by noon. We were sitting side by side on a log with our backs to a tree line, facing a small field. We had been sitting quietly for about twenty minutes, taking our lunch break, when we heard something momentarily rustling behind us and off to our left in the trees.

I had turned my head to look and saw nothing. My wife had done the same as we continued to eat. I don't mean to sound like hearing something rustling is any big deal, as there is so much wildlife in here, but every noise does, and should, get your attention when hiking. The two of us have stumbled across many a bear, and even a cougar, during our many hikes. A few minutes later, as I was pulling my nasal inhaler out of my pocket, we heard what sounded like a loud crack, followed by the sound of a tree dragging on the ground; at least, that's what I thought at the time.

The two of us stood up from our seat on the log and turned to face the woods in the direction of the noise, with the trees being maybe seventy-five feet, at best, in front of us. From the position we were in, you couldn't really see into the trees to our left or to our right hand side, but there was a small opening directly in front of us. We continued to look and listen as this sound of something dragging seemed to be getting closer and louder. Suddenly, a Bigfoot appeared from behind the trees to our right, walking into this opening and dragging a small tree in its right hand. As soon as it had made its way past the barrier of the trees and into the opening, it turned its face to look at us and dropped the tree that was in its hand. Turning to the right, it slowly started to walk towards the rear of the opening, retreating back into the woods. It craned its neck, looking back at us as it walked away, before it completely disappeared from view.

I don't think it was but five minutes after we had seen it that we moved forward to where it had dropped the tree. Edna and I stood there looking at the tree. It was dead, but considerably large to be dragging around. It must have been easily thirty feet long and was about six inches in diameter at the base. Why this creature was dragging this particular tree, and to where, is anyone's guess. Our own thoughts being, at the time, that it couldn't have been planning to take it very far or else it would have grabbed another tree nearer to that location. It must have been going to or living somewhere in close proximity to where we were standing.

I am sure that this Bigfoot was as surprised to see us as we were to see it, perhaps even more so. I say this because we had a fair warning, having heard it coming. To me, there was absolutely no fear exhibited by the beast when it saw us. Having seen the size of it, the reason why is more than evident. We had a more than perfect view of it for some thirty seconds or more. When we walked over to look at the tree it had been dragging, there were several boughs that we had watched it pass behind as it walked, all of which were in the neighborhood of eight to nine feet off the ground. This was one big mother; I can tell you that emphatically. It appeared to be almost jet black with some red highlights that were shining in the sunlight as it broke into the small clearing.

From the side, it seemed to be about three feet thick, from front to back, and its fingers on the left hand were hanging just below knee level. One of the oddities about it was that the head looked tiny for the body. Now don't get me wrong, the musculature was immense in every sense of the word, but even at that, the head seemed relatively small. We couldn't really make out any muscular definition other than that everywhere you looked, the body seemed to be bulging outward, such as the chest and the back. It was, quite obviously, built strongly to the extreme. It was casually walking holding this tree in one hand that, even dead, had to have weighed at least a couple of hundred pounds or more. The other thing about the sighting which I can't forget is the leisurely way in which, after it had seen us, it walked away. There was absolutely no sense of fear or urgency on its part after having seen us. I guess it knows that it could tear us limb from limb if it had to. At any rate, that was our sighting of "The Red Buttes Beast," as we named him.

My dear readers…some six months after Mitchell was interviewed about the encounter at Red Buttes, I received a phone call from none other than Mitchell himself. It seems that Mitchell had a bit of an update which he wanted to share with me and you. Here is what Mitchell had to say:

I guess you were surprised to hear from me again, but I just couldn't let a sleeping dog rest. I had been troubled since the day of the encounter as to what the Bigfoot was doing, dragging the tree around in the woods, and had decided to go back into the area to do a little investigating. My wife, Edna, wanted nothing to do with it, so I brought along my best friend, Larry, who was more than interested after having heard about our encounter. The two of us made our way in exactly as my wife and I had on that day. I knew I was at the precise location of the last sighting because I had dropped and forgotten about my nasal inhaler, only to find it lying next to the log where we had eaten our lunch.

The first thing that we did was to step into the opening where we had seen the beast leave the tree. It was gone. This immediately indicated to me that this Bigfoot was all business and had come back to finish what he had started after we had left. Larry and I began to do a very methodical search, expanding outward at about twenty yards at a time, working our way into the woods where the creature was heading. Our hope was to discover what the tree was being taken for without ending up dead in the process. By the way, we had both brought our handguns with us on this trip.

I guess it was about two hours into this grid search that we ran across a teepee like structure made of trees in the woods. There must have been well over fifty trees set to lean against some horizontal branches of one large living tree. As we walked around this structure, if you can believe it, I actually remembered and recognized the bark pattern on the one that he had dropped and saw it within this structure. As we stood there examining this phenomena, Larry said that he thought he saw something dark out of the corner of his eye and pointed in the direction he wanted me to look. Neither of us could see anything, but he was certain that he had seen some dark color move in, and through, a small opening in the branches.

Now, Larry is a very able and experienced woodsman; if he says he saw something, he most definitely did. "Dark color," in these parts, means bear and, perhaps, during this venture, a Bigfoot. Needless to say, you don't start wandering around looking for either with handguns. Well, we had a lot to talk about and began our hike back out. We must have hiked two miles or more, bullshitting the whole time about what we had just seen and what my wife and I had seen previously. I could tell that Larry had caught the bug, just as I had. There is something quite extraordinary that happens to a man or woman when you see one of these creatures. Speaking for myself, it is now like I can't let it go; I want to know more and I want to see more.

Anyways, so we are hiking about two miles outbound from the structure when, unexpectedly, a large and voluminous howl starts emanating from the woods coming directly from where we had been. We both turned to listen and it must have went on for almost twenty seconds before it stopped. It was louder than the blast of a cruise ship's horn and it made our hair stand on end. I said to Larry that the Bigfoot must have been giving us a farewell salute. There was absolutely nothing else in this region that the sound could have been coming from.

Well now, my dear readers, it seems that Larry found himself engaged in a bit of a doubleheader, so to speak. That was really quite remarkable, indeed.

Taken

The following story is one of those that had been received and told to me with such sincerity and intensity that I had to pass it along to you, the reader. It's not always what is seen that can send a chill down one's spine, as you will soon find out for yourself. You will now be hearing the story as it was told to me by Tim Strong, a resident of the state of Virginia.

As I told you before, Bill, this story scared the living shit out of me when I first heard it. I thought it would be something that you may well be interested in, so here goes nothing. My friend and co-worker, Roberto, and I were doing a four day hike through the Shenandoah National Park in Virginia. Along this Appalachian Trail, there are actually some accommodations in place for the weary hikers. There are small, locked, trailside cabins which can be reserved in advance, located in several locations. They contain bunks, mattresses, blankets, cooking utensils, and many other necessities.

In addition, there are many three-sided shelters in which there are bunks and an outdoor fireplace for warmth and cooking. It is relative to one of these three-sided structures that our story will unfold. Now these three-sided shelters are a shared commodity. In other words, if you are in there and a couple of other hikers come along to crash for the night, you are obligated to welcome them in and make the best of it. Everyone deserves shelter for the night and it may be many miles before coming across another one on the trail. So Roberto and I, having planned to make it to this certain shelter for the night, had arrived at the location finding it already occupied by a husband and wife.

Having made all of our apologies for having nowhere else to crash for the night, they said that there were no apologies needed. In fact, they said, "We are rather happy that you came by because some strange happenings have gone on here and we weren't looking forward to being here alone tonight." Naturally, the question arose, "What exactly are the strange happenings of which you speak?"

Before I continue, let me say that these are in fact three sided shelters. They have a roof with two sides and a back and one side being completely open to whoever, and whatever, may come along. We were, by the way, spending the night in the shelter by Loft Mountain. The couple went on to tell us that some two years ago, a group of four hikers was doing exactly what we were doing, just south of us in the shelter by Big Flat Mountain. Upon awaking in the morning, one of group of four was no longer in the shelter. Her backpack was left behind. The couple went on to say that over a period of days, a large search had been undertaken for the missing girl that came up empty. It was some several weeks later, near the border of West Virginia many miles away from the location of the disappearance, that a man walking through the woods came upon the body of the girl draped over the upper limb of a large tree, naked and having been partially dismembered.

After they had told us this story, I couldn't sleep a wink during the night. In the morning, as we got about the business of resuming our hike, my friend Roberto, who is a half mad rebel from Central America, gets the bone-headed idea that we should go south and spend the night at the very shelter where this event had taken place two years ago. I told him he was out of his mind, but after much back and forth about it being a freaky thing to do and this and that, I had succumbed to the plan and off we went.

Having arrived there, it was basically a duplicate of where we had been last night; only this night, he and I were alone. As the sun set and the evening turned into the night, I had basically been up for well over twenty-four hours, having not slept at all during the night. To be quite honest with you, I wasn't too keen on falling asleep there that night. It must have been around midnight when I looked at Roberto and he was sound asleep. This guy could fall asleep during a blizzard sitting on a curb and yet I was still awake. It wasn't just that we had heard the story about what happened here, but to me there was most certainly some type of creepy residual aspect about being here.

I was uncomfortable the entire night, feeling as though we were being watched; by whom or what, I can't tell you, but I just couldn't shake it. Speaking for myself, the sun couldn't come up soon enough and I was sorry that I had listened to Roberto's rant about wanting to come here. He was asleep and I was being mentally tortured for the entire night in the shelter. Nothing had happened during the night and we commenced to finish our hike in the morning. The question which lingers to this day in my mind, and I would guess in the minds of many others…the question which was the reason for my contacting you in the first place is this: exactly who or what is capable of taking a human being many miles away, only to dismember them and put them up in a tree for safe keeping? That's what really blew my mind about this whole affair.

My dear readers, in my first book, Bigfoot: Terror in the Woods: Sightings and Encounters, Volume 1, *one of my witnesses had sighted a Bigfoot in this very same area, charging and killing a black bear that was feeding on a deer carcass. Absolutely incredible!*

The Glacier Creek Sighting

The following account was told to me by Sharon Higgins, who was
fly fishing with her guide and friend, Tommy Rheinbeck:

I know that I had told you that Tommy was my guide on this day
when we saw the Bigfoot, but the reality is that he is also my best
friend and companion, who just happens to have introduced me to
fly fishing and many of his favorite haunts. On this particular day,
we had hiked into the Bear Lake region of the Rocky Mountain National Park, and had begun to survey the shoreline of Glacier Creek
looking for any brook trout on the rise. As we were walking through
the brush alongside of the creek, we came upon somewhat of a break
that opened up into a beaver dam. There seemed to be quite a bit of
activity going on, as we could see the brookies plucking some type of
hatch off the surface. We decided that this was as good a spot as any
to cast our flies. We found a little spot where we could cozy up to the
brush, but still make a decent back swing, and began to fish.

Standing where we were on the shore, I would estimate that it was about a hundred yards or so to the other side of the creek. There, we were looking at what I will describe as three tiers of greenery. The first level, which began against the creek, was tall, bright green grass that I would say was about three feet tall or so. This grass ran away from the creek for some thirty feet where it met up with the second tier, which was comprised of scrubby bushes and short trees being between, say, five and fifteen feet tall. This tier ran further away from the creek for, maybe, another twenty yards or so, where it abutted what appeared to be a forest of either spruce or fir trees that were, more than likely, forty to sixty feet tall.

Our vision to our right hand side was completely obscured by the trees flanking us on the bank. The same situation was visible on the other side of the bank, to the left of this three-tier-thing that I just described. In other words, this tier setup was not going along the whole creek. It was only visible for a width of maybe 200 yards or so on the opposing bank, if that makes any sense. We had been fishing there, quietly, for maybe two hours, when I began to see something moving within this second tier of low bushes and trees on the other bank. I would see some dark fur and then it would disappear from view within these bushes. This had occurred three or four times, already, and I had directed Tommy to look in the direction of what I was seeing. As we stood there watching for any further activity by whatever this was concealed within the bushes, a figure suddenly emerged from behind the trees alongside of the grass and started walking through the grass along the edge of the creek.

As I told you, I believe the grass that we were looking at was about three feet tall and, perhaps, even more. This grass was just about covering this creatures legs up to the knees. The two of us knew immediately that we were looking at a Bigfoot and there was no doubt about it. As I recall, it had only taken two steps as it came from behind the bushes into the grass, when it turned its head looking directly at us. I could see the sunlight illuminating its face. Without missing a single step, it kept its gaze upon us for maybe ten more paces. The creature then turned its face looking straight ahead once again as it continued to walk through the grass. At no point in time did it stop or change the cadence of its walk. It simply realized we were there; giving us the once over and kept walking. It continued walking for the entire width of this grassy area and then, once again, was concealed behind the trees to our right hand side.

We both stood there in utter awe and amazement at what we had just seen with our very own eyes. Not in our wildest dreams did we think that such a thing would happen to us, and yet it just had. Even at 150 or 200 yards, the size of this beast was staggering. Based on the height of the grass, it must have been some ten feet tall, or so. To the human eye, it appeared to be going very slowly, almost gliding, and yet it had covered a large amount of ground in a very brief amount of time. I could only imagine what it could do if it was running. Its movements were so smooth and fluid-like that it's hard to describe to anyone having not been there for themselves.

We could tell that the face had very little, if any, fur on it, and we could tell that it had a forward lean to its walk, with its head being positioned maybe a foot or so ahead of what we would call its waist line. Of course, as everyone has already heard, its arms were ridiculously long and swung in practically perfect timing with each step that it took. To me, it almost looked as though they had to move in this fashion in order for it to walk. I know that seems very strange, but there almost appeared to be some type of connection going on between the arms and legs as it walked. At any rate, there you have it. That was the entirety of my Bigfoot sighting at Glacier Creek in July of 2016.

The Shadow Mountain Sighting

This account was told to me by Susan Paterson, who was on a hike in the Rocky Mountain National Park with her girlfriends at the time. Here is what Susan had to say:

On the day I had my sighting, my girlfriends and I had decided to take a hike up to the fire lookout station atop Shadow Mountain. The hike began from the Grand Lake entrance area. We soon found ourselves wrapping around the lake, with Shadow Mountain in full view.

In hindsight, I would highly recommend wearing bug spray when walking near the lake. It was something that we did not have that day, and boy, did we pay for it! The mosquitoes were absolutely brutal, at times, as we were close to the water's edge. Once we were clear of the area, we started heading directly towards the mountain itself and its ascending trail. By the time we were midway up the mountain trail, we had already seen a bear and several deer, as well as many chipmunks and what I believe was a mink, or something of the sort.

Once you are beyond the midway point, the trail becomes quite steep. There were a lot of trees across the trail that day, which made things quite difficult for us. Nevertheless, we had made it to the top. We approached the lookout with relief, but were disappointed. To our dismay, the tower's staircase was locked, keeping us from climbing up into it. Basically, it's a fairly short tower made from stone, with painted brown logs forming a deck base on the top; upon which a small, hut-like structure is attached to it. So, we sat up there for about an hour or two, enjoying the views from every side of the mountain. It was actually breathtaking and I would highly recommend it to anyone with a good pair of legs.

The trees in this area are predominantly some type of narrow-growing pines, which I believe are spruce. A fair amount of them are dead, which creates a type of screen to the eyes as you are peering about on the trail. We had actually seen bears and deer walking about in this timber screening as we were on our way up to the lookout station. It gave the appearance of something walking behind a stockade fence, with every other slat removed. What I am trying to do here is to set the stage for you visually for what we were about to see on our descent from Shadow Mountain.

The three of us had just passed the steepest section as we were making our way down the slope. It was right about that time when my girlfriend, Tricia, said, "Look, guys, there's another bear down there!"

As we all turned our heads to look, I think that Tricia realized at the same time that we all did that this wasn't a bear, but rather a Bigfoot. At first glance, this was an easy mistake to make because of the broken field of vision created by all of the dead grey trees.

We were quite a bit higher than this creature that was walking through the trees down and away off to our righthand side. We weren't making any noise, other than walking; otherwise, I am sure it would have spied us out, but it hadn't. This Bigfoot was on a mission because it didn't stop for a second as it was walking. When we first saw it, I believe we were maybe three or four hundred feet away from it and we were able to get some fairly good looks at it as it traversed the slope. The only way it could have seen us would have been to look up and over its left shoulder, which it, thankfully, didn't do. At the place we were on the trail, there was really nowhere to hide, so we just quietly stood our ground and watched. This thing was moving very quickly through the tightly packed pines, and we could see the tree tops rocking back and forth as it parted them, making its way through using its arms and hands to clear the path. I would say that most of the trees in here were between, say, twelve and twenty five feet tall. The Bigfoot measured up as being pretty damn tall, in our estimation. It was an incredible sight to behold, and no, it wasn't a man in a monkey suit.

One of the most bothersome things about having a sighting like this is the after effect of how you are received by your peers, having told them of your experience. Speaking for myself, I was as high as a kite for weeks after the sighting, and anxious to tell everyone and anyone about what I had seen, but those euphoric feelings soon dwindled away as I saw and heard the reactions of those with whom I spoke. It's really a crying shame that people choose to be so ignorant about these things. However, that's coming from someone's perspective who had just seen one. I am not sure how I would have reacted had you told me of your experience, but I'd like to think that I would have responded in a better way than most.

The Lake Solitude Sighting

This brief, but telling, sighting was told to me by Brandon Richards, a resident of the state of Colorado. Here is was Brandon had to say:

My friend, Anthony, and I had planned to spend five days backpacking and camping in the Grand Teton National Park. During the course of the first three days, we had been working our way into and through a variety of locations within the park. It was on the fourth day that we found ourselves sitting at a higher elevation, overlooking Lake Solitude below us in the valley, with the western slope of Grand Teton facing us in the distance. From our vantage point, which was considerable, both of the slopes descending down to the lake were in view. They were sporadically covered with large swaths of pine trees. This was a vast, panoramic view which I am attempting to paint for the mind's eye, just so you can better understand what I am speaking about. When you see something in the distance here, it is extremely difficult to judge just how far that distance is. Everything is much further away then it appears; a fact which becomes more than evident once you begin hiking towards what you are seeing.

We were perched on this low mountainside overlooking what I just described to you, taking in the view. The two of us each carried a good pair of field glasses, which we had not needed up until the moment Anthony's focus fixated on something below us.

He reached into his backpack for his binoculars and raised them to his eyes, not saying a word. As he began to look intently at what appeared to be a very specific location, he told me to grab my binoculars and focus in on what he was looking at. I said to Anthony, "What do you see?" He responded, "Just grab your glasses and look between those two groups of trees down there to the right." I did as he said and started to scan the area of which he spoke when suddenly I said, "It's a damn Bigfoot!" Anthony said to me, "I know…I just wanted to hear what you would say to confirm what I already thought." There was no doubt about it.

The two of us now had our lenses fixed clearly on a large, black beast walking on two legs in and out of the trees on the slope well below us. The distance could have been at the very least a mile or more. However, with the twenty by fifty binoculars, we had an extremely good field of view, which included the Bigfoot and its activities. Now, it's not that I need to explain my somewhat instantaneous response of it being a Bigfoot, but it was painfully obvious what we were seeing.

First of all, there is never anyone seen hiking or hunting in these parts dressed from head to toe in black and wearing no shoes or boots. Secondly, there would be, under no circumstances, anyone in this area without a backpack and supplies just casually sauntering around in the wilderness. Third, there is literally and figuratively nobody out here, especially where we were. In the three days prior, we had sighted a group of three individuals that were more than likely half a mile away from us coming off a ridge and that was it, as far as human contact is concerned.

As we sat watching the Bigfoot walking through our lenses, it suddenly stopped. As it was facing one of the pines, it began to do something with its arms extended. It was using its hands in a way which made it appear as though it was working on or picking at the side of the pine. We watched him doing this for well over a half an hour. Occasionally, we could see the beast crouch or bend down to the ground where it appeared to be picking something up that had fallen to the ground. The beast would then follow this action by putting its hand to its face or mouth. I don't need to tell you that at this distance, we couldn't see any details at all.

After the creature had spent a considerable amount of time by the side of this tree, it started to move around, in and out of our field of vision. It appeared to be looking at some other trees that were near to it. My recollection is that we had lost sight of it for about for-ty-five minutes when it emerged from the trees and started walking along the slope, heading away from us and toward Lake Solitude. Now, just to settle the score with those who think that people who see such a thing are suffering from some type of delusional disorder, this was like looking at a jet-black Frankenstein walking in the mid-dle of nowhere. Even at the distance from which we were watching, the creature walked with the long arm swings and the deliberate lengthy strides. These dramatic movements were more than obvi-ous to the eye, but this thing was not putting on a show for anyone to see; we were more than a mile away watching it from an elevation of well over a thousand feet or more. It had no idea that it was being watched by anyone or anything. With all the various stories that the two of us, and so many others, have heard about these things through the years, this sighting had completely sealed the deal for Anthony and I. Bigfoot is, in fact, the real deal!

The Hen House

This simple, yet telling, encounter was told to me by John and Barbara Small, who are residents of Pennsylvania. Here is what they had to say:

My wife and I had purchased a house that was listed as, "For Sale by Owner," in the western Pennsylvania area. It was an all-cash deal with a fast closing. When we went to look at the house, the couple who were living there had a beat up, little shack in the backyard. The main house was so nice that I couldn't believe they had this piece-of-garbage building in the backyard. It was painted barn red and looked like it had been repaired ten times over with chewing gum and band aids. It was, however, being actively used by them as a hen house. The access door on the end of the house looked like it was hanging on by a thread. It was held shut by a piece of clothesline that was nailed to the wood on one end and wrapped around a boat cleat on the other.

Along the one long side of this shack, the upper half of the exterior sheathing had been removed, exposing the stud wall. This was covered now in chicken wire that had been stapled in place. The bottom side of this same wall had a hole cut in it for the hens to go in and out. Along the outside edge was a pen made of pressure treated four by four lumber and chicken wire. It was the most ramshackle, junk box set-up I had ever seen. Two weeks before we closed the deal, they asked my wife and I if we wanted them to leave the chickens for us, to which we replied, "No, thank you," and we left it at that.

At the closing table in the attorney's office, we had asked them during some small talk how they made out with the removal of the chickens. John, the husband, said, "Thank God, we got rid of them at the last minute only yesterday afternoon."

The following day, my wife and I were over there painting the interior of the house. My friend, Lou, was prepping the bathroom for a new tile job. Less than six days later, we had moved in. It was on the evening of April 26, 2015, three days after we had moved in, that all hell broke loose. I remember the exact date because we had just celebrated my wife's first birthday in the new home on the twenty-fifth. During the last stages of twilight, after the sun had already set for the day, I stepped out the back door onto the patio having just come home from work. All of the following things that I am about to say to you virtually happened at the same time:

As I stepped out of the back door, my eyes were immediately drawn to the rope lock on the hen house. It was unraveled, leaving the door open on the now empty coop. As I was looking at this open door, I had pulled the door shut hard behind me, quite loudly, when without warning, a Bigfoot launched outward from inside of the coop! He jumped out in what I would call a "Superman leap" straight through the chicken wire, which was now wrapped around him as he landed on the ground. He was gigantic and came flying out in full force, completely horizontal to the ground, landing on all fours maybe twenty-five feet from the coop. With one swift movement, he stood to his feet, flinging both of his arms into the air, throwing the wire off his body. He turned, snarled at me, and then, he literally launched himself into the woods behind our home in what was maybe three consecutive leaps. I wouldn't call them steps because the amount of ground he had covered in these three movements of his legs was insane.

All of this had happened so quickly that I didn't even have time to think about what was unfolding before my very own eyes. It momentarily felt like my heart had stopped and I wasn't breathing. If he had wanted to get me, I would have been dead meat for sure, but it seemed like I had surprised the monster and it just wanted to get the heck out of our yard. I have never in my life been that close to anything remotely as large as this thing was. It became immediately obvious to me that it was familiar with the smell and location of this house, which did, by the way, stink like chicken shit. And I was left wondering if it hadn't been here before. When he stood up in front of me, he looked like one giant cube of animal. It reminded me of the old Hulk T.V. show, when Bill what's-his-name transformed into the monster. The Bigfoot was totally ripped up in every sense of the word, being just muscle upon muscle.

He had the most evil looking facial grimace that you could ever imagine. When he growled at me, his upper lip somewhat receded as he showed me his teeth. As he did this this, his facial skin kind of scrunched up, forming large layer of wrinkles up to his eyes, which were completely black. I could see that the underlying skin was dark gray in color. Initially I had thought that he was completely covered in hair, but he was not. He did have somewhat of what I will call a beard, and there was actually quite a bit of hair on his face, with the exception of the area on both sides of his nose. To me, his ears seemed too small for his head, and they were flush to the sides as well.

My wife, who works in a local hospital until 11 p.m., could not believe what I told her when she came home. Quite frankly, who could blame her? It was the craziest and most frightening event of my life to date, and I hope that I never have to endure it again.

Well, my dear readers, I cannot begin to tell you how many people have contacted me with similar stories, about the animals in and around their homes being taken by these creatures. They are most certainly opportunistic and will in no way pass up a free meal if it is presented to them.

The McDonald Creek Footbridge Sighting

This brief sighting was brought to my attention by Edward Bernstein and his wife, Chloe, who were hiking in the vicinity of Lake McDonald within Glacier National Park. Here is what they saw:

Chloe and I had been out for a day hike in Glacier National when we found ourselves approaching the McDonald Creek Footbridge. Now, why they call this a creek is beyond me, because it's actually quite wide, and there is white water in every direction that you look. Chloe and I were standing in the middle of the bridge, taking in the sights and sounds of the creek, and absorbing the beauty of the day. We must have been standing there for about a half an hour when we decided to continue our little trek, crossing over the remainder of the bridge, and making our way into the trail.

As you crossover the bridge, the trail continues along the lower side of what I will call a small mountain, which is covered in pines that continue up the sides of its steep slope. We were just breaking into the trail, having crossed the footbridge, when Chloe said to me, "Ed what is that over there?"

As my eyes became fixed on where she was now pointing, I could see a large, fur covered creature peering out from behind a tree only, maybe, fifty feet or so away from us. This creature was at least four or five times wider than the tree it was hiding behind, and it kept moving its head behind and then away from the tree, looking directly at us when it did so. It was enormous in stature and Chloe had grabbed my arm in fear. As soon as I saw it, I knew that I was looking at a Bigfoot. It was repeating this movement of going behind the tree and then looking back at us so quickly, that it was hard to keep track of how many times it had actually occurred.

The tree it was standing behind was no more than, say, fourteen inches wide, and there was at least a foot or more of its body visible on both sides. In the moment, I remember thinking that it must have been watching us on the bridge, and perhaps we caught it off guard as we quickly resumed our hike going in the direction it was standing. At any rate, it seemed very nervous, which was something I was not too happy about. If it had decided to come at us and do us harm, there would have been little or nothing that we could have done to defend ourselves against it. It was all of eight or nine feet tall and extremely broad. Each time that it tilted or leaned away from the tree, its left hand remained on the side of the trunk while the rest of the body came into view. Its mouth was shut the entire time and it didn't make as much as a sound. The face was very flat as far as we could see and its expression was very mean or evil looking, although it wasn't exhibiting any behavior to match its appearance.

What I just described to you was going on for maybe a minute, when it turned and started to move up the slope on an angle going away from us. This was a very steep incline that was densely packed with trees, yet each of the steps it took appeared to be something like ten feet long. The Bigfoot was totally out of our sight in about five strides, having covered some forty or fifty feet into the trees. We could hear some crunching noises for maybe another thirty seconds and then, there was nothing.

My wife and I immediately retreated back over the bridge and high-tailed it out of there. Chloe was visibly shaking and I guess I was in somewhat of a state of shock. I remember I was breathing very shallowly and was having trouble gathering my thoughts about what had just occurred. As far as what this Bigfoot looked like, as I just said, at the waist alone, it was at least three to four feet wide, and then its body tapered outward from there. I would have to estimate that at the outside edges of its shoulders, we are talking at the very least, six to seven feet or so. It was absolutely staggering to the eyes. Its face was mostly covered in hair, with the exception being around, and just below, its eyes as well as part of the cheek area.

Its fingers, that were wrapped around the tree's trunk, were very long; perhaps, almost a foot in length. What we would call the pectoral muscles made it appear like there were two bed pillows plastered to its upper chest. The thickness of its biceps were at least ten inches or more. When it stepped away from us, I could see the bottoms of its feet briefly on, maybe, two of the steps that it had taken. From my perspective, they appeared to be grey and somewhat flat, like the sole of a well-worn shoe. I distinctly remember the nose being extremely broad and flat to the face, which made the lower jaw seem to be protrude abnormally from the face. My hope is that I have done a good job in reporting this sighting to you and your readers. Having said as much, mere words cannot and will not ever take the place of having the encounter for yourself. It was a combination of total fear and total ecstasy at the same time; kind of like finding a pot of gold that could kill you.

Well, my dear readers, it seems like the Boogers like the parks as much as we do, and maybe more so. I recall back sometime in the seventies, if I am not mistaken, that there was a big deal being made over logging in the Pacific Northwest somewhere. The story at the time being told that we were destroying the habitat of some type of owl and they wanted it to stop. With many years having past and in hindsight, I wonder if it wasn't something else's habitat that they were trying to protect in order to keep them in check, so to speak. Anyway, it's just a thought.

The Mount Revelstoke Encounter

This encounter was brought to my attention by Gunther Henkel, a resident of Boulder Colorado. Here is what Gunther had to say about his encounter:

It was July of 2009 that my wife, Hilda, and I had gone to spend a week in Mount Revelstoke National Park to take in a little relaxation and some hiking. We had planned our vacation around the summer months when the alpine meadows are in full bloom, being carpeted with yellow arnica, asters, blue lupine, scarlet paint brush and the white valerians. It very much reminds us of our youth in Germany. We had begun our day's hike from the campground near the Lindmark Trail, our destination being the meadow atop Revelstoke at some 6,300 feet. On the lower slope, we were making our way through the mountain ash, green elders, wild cherries, red and black elders, and the black cottonwoods. Interspersed with all of these are huckleberry, blueberry, and salmon berry bushes, which attract quite a few bears, so you must be careful.

As you ascend the slope the Douglas fir, giant cedar, and white pine start to takeover. After some four or five thousand feet, it is the Engelmann spruce and alpine firs that dominate the landscape. Having made the summit, we had entered into what is a rolling alpine meadow, with Mount Tilley and Mount Mackenzie being in full view in the distance.

Spruce and firs are scattered in patches and small groupings here at the summit. We had sat down on some small boulders for a well needed rest after the climb. I think we had been sitting for maybe a half hour in the sun, when Hilda pointed out to me that one of the spruce trees, some two or three hundred yards away from our position, was thrashing back and forth in a violent, and most unusual, fashion. We sat watching this for some ten minutes or so, fully expecting to see a bear emerge from the trees. When nothing of the sort happened, we continued to watch and wait. The tree, having stopped shaking, Hilda and I decided to move a bit closer in hopes of seeing some type of wildlife in the trees. I think we had advanced perhaps fifty yards or so when a loud sound, what I will describe as a violent roar, erupted from the grouping of trees directly ahead of us.

This was the same patch where the one tree had been shaking violently only minutes before. This roar was so loud that I could feel the pressure from it in my body; despite us being some two hundred yards away from its origin. At least, that was my estimation at the time. Neither of us had ever heard a grizzly roar and we both believed that this was in fact what we had heard. The roar had frozen us in our tracks and we actually started to slowly retreat when a large, hairy beast on two legs came running out of the trees some fifty yards and stopped abruptly in the meadow. It was looking directly at us, flailing it arms around in the air and thrashing its head and upper body back and forth while growling. The growl sounded more like a deep, guttural whine. The speed with which this beast had run the fifty yards was so fast that, if it had continued, it would have been on us in a matter of seconds. That would have been our demise, for certain.

I grabbed Hilda's hand and we slowly started to back away, not wanting to startle the beast. As we did so, it made yet another fast charge towards us, once again stopping after some twenty or thirty yards. This charge was followed yet again by the growling and flailing of the arms and head just as it had done on the first charge. The size of this thing was immense and its actions told us that its intent was vicious, to say the least. The two of us kept slowly backing away as the beast was intermittently continuing to growl and throw its arms and head around in front of us. We had actually backed away some seventy five yards or so, when the two of us turned and started to walk. At first, our steps were slow and cautious and then, we quickened our pace, making it over the side of the meadow to head back down the slope of Revelstoke. As my wife and I made our descent from the meadow, we couldn't help thinking that this creature was going to follow us over the side at some point. We were on edge.

Finally, we had reached the bottom, and when we were well clear of the trees, the two of us sat down for a well-deserved break and began to talk. Both of us now knew we had encountered a Bigfoot and thought that, in some way, shape, or form, we had walked in on some type of activity it was planning in this meadow atop Revelstoke. We had become intruders in its territory and it wasn't happy about us being there. Although it could have easily crossed the entire meadow and attacked us, it didn't; which indicated to us that it was trying to scare us off. It had done one heck of a job in doing so!

Being so far away from us, it is hard to say how big it really was, having nothing to measure it against. The thing that impressed me most was the depth of its roar. It had to have come from deep within the bowels of a very substantial beast indeed. The second thing was how quickly it was able to move with relative ease. During both of the charges towards us, it was able to cover a large amount of ground in what appeared to be six or eight very rapid steps. They appeared to be fast leaps that were very hard to distinguish separately. The succession of these leaps was so quick that to our eyes, it seemed like a blur. However tall it may have been, its physique was that of a body builder. It was fully covered in a reddish- brown hair that appeared to be somewhere between say, four and ten inches long, depending on the area of the body you looked at.

This encounter was so dramatic and life changing that we just had to tell you about it. Seeing is certainly believing, and neither of us had really given much thought to the reality of their existence until that day in the meadow; how quickly things change.

The 1956 Muir Woods Sighting

The following sighting was brought to my attention by retired professor, Richard Hayes, a young man of seventy-nine years of age. Here is what the good Professor had to say:

As I told you when we first spoke, Bill, that I was a professor of biological studies for almost forty years, when I finally decided to call it quits. Although what I am about to say to you and your readers is actually quite dated, it rings true to the foreword you had in your first book, which is how I came to know you. In your foreword, you said rather concisely that, "people see because they are looking." To that rather poignant point, I must commend you, for this is exactly what I have been prodding my students to do my entire career. If I said it once, I said it a thousand times that we need to open our eyes to the beauty that surrounds us, wherever we may find ourselves. There is so much to see and so few who see it. It is in this same light, that my wife and I came to see the Bigfoot long before the name became somewhat commonplace.

In my earlier years, I, like you, was an observer of all things. I would regularly take long hikes, either alone or in the company of my wife after we had met. On this particular day, which was June 23, 1956, my wife and I had gone into the Muir Woods National Monument, which is a protected, cathedral-like grove of virgin redwoods located in a valley north of San Francisco. So you and your readers can understand, the area of which I speak was an entirely different place at the time when we were there, as opposed to now. There was not a fraction of the people and habitations that one can see in the region today.

As a little science lesson, which I think that you and your readers can appreciate, many people often confuse the coastal redwoods with the giant sequoia of the Sierra. Both belong to the genus *Sequoia,* but are separate species of that genus. The species that grows in the Muir Woods is *Sequoia sempervirens*, which is more commonly called the redwood. The species which grows in the Sierra Nevada at altitudes between four and eight thousand feet is *Sequoia gigantean*, more commonly known as the giant sequoia. Redwoods can live about two thousand years, while the giant sequoias can exceed three thousand years or more. Many of these trees were alive when Christ was put on the cross, to bring this into perspective. My wife and I had begun our hike from the parking lot on the main trail. At the time, it was the park's policy that nobody was to leave the trail. We began the hike on what was known as the Nature Trail, which brought us into an area of redwoods known as the Bohemian Grove.

When we exited the grove, we had crossed Redwood Creek and proceeded up the Main Trail towards what was known as Cathedral Grove; a distance which was perhaps a half mile or so. Now, to the unlearned, one might think that you would be walking through a woods comprised of telephone poles, with visibility being grand in every direction, but such is not the case. The forest is predominantly quite shady and there are actually many varieties of trees and bushes competing for the sunlight in the base of the forest. That, in conjunction with the quantity and width of the redwoods, made for a more tunnel- like effect on the trail in most locations. You could not see very far ahead or to your right or left hand.

The two of us were alone and well along on the trail, when we stopped to look at a California variety of fetid adderstongue, growing by the base of one of the redwoods. This is a rather unique plant variety and it caught our eye. As the two of us were bent over examining this plant species, the view ahead of us on the trail looked somewhat like a keyhole formed by the trees. We were touching the plant and talking about its beauty when, out of the corner of my eye, I saw something dart across the trail beyond this keyhole that I just described to you. Whatever it was had crossed the trail on two legs, maybe 150 to 200 feet ahead of us. I told my wife that I thought I had just seen a man cross the path up ahead of us, but that I was uncertain. My wife replied, "Let's go and have a look see."

As we were walking ahead, we heard a distinct *Whoop! Whoop!* The noise came from within the forest to our left. From our perspective you couldn't see a thing except branches, bushes, and tree trunks. There wasn't a soul in sight. My wife and I had both said that no one was supposed to go off the trail into the woods, so who exactly had done this we did not know. Upon reaching the spot where I saw the man go across the trail, there was somewhat of an opening in the trees, looking back into the forest for quite some distance. As we stood there, peering through this picture frame like view, going back deep into the trees, A large, hairy, gorilla-like creature leaned out from behind a redwood, and quickly moved back behind it.

My wife said to me, "My word, Richard, what on earth was that? Did you see it?"

I had seen exactly what she had. It was what appeared to be an eight foot tall gorilla. Keeping in mind that at that time, there were no discussions about Bigfoot or Sasquatch and the like. We had never heard of such a thing, neither had we read any material whatsoever in any of the scientific publications about them. We had simply observed something that we were trying to label and the term *gorilla* fit the bill. The tree it was hiding behind had enormous girth and we could see nothing of it. My wife said that she was frightened and that she wanted to leave. As I was trying to comfort her and get her to stay for just a few more minutes, this gorilla walked out from behind the tree and back into the forest, out of our sight.

The two of us, to be quite frank with you, were completely baffled by what we had seen. As the creature walked away, its back was turned to us and it had briefly turned its upper body to give us a glance. At that moment, its skin looked grey on the face and it had a very broad jawline. The face was completely devoid of hair as far I can remember. The overall dimensions of the creature's body were staggering. Its body was so wide that had it been hiding behind anything less than a redwood, we would have seen it. Its thighs and legs were so thick, that I soon realized as I saw it that it must have been further than I thought when I first saw it out of the corner of my eye.

I asked Richard to expound upon any other details other than what he had said and here is what he added:

The fur appeared to be a mix of dark brown and red. This coloration was only visible for a brief moment as it walked through a solitary ray of sunlight, gleaming down through the canopy. When it turned its head to look at us, it didn't really turn its head, but rather its entire upper body. I knew why after it had turned back away from us. The head was actually tucked in forward to the shoulders, because as it walked away, the enormous muscles of its upper back concealed most of the head. It apparently couldn't just turn its head around without the whole body following.

The shoulder width must have been every bit of five to six feet. It wasn't until that film had made headlines years later that we now knew what we had seen, and what he had filmed. This creature was very similar to the one in the film, only more lean and muscular. Again, Bill, I must complement you on your foreword, which was pure genius, in which you simply stated that people know what they are seeing without any contributing notions coming from anyone else.

Well, my dear readers, if the Professor knows what a fetid adderstongue is, then I think he knows if and when he sees a Bigfoot. Your thoughts?

Death From Above

This extremely gruesome account was told to me by Todd Schyling, who, at the time, hailed from the area of Takoma Washington. Here is what Todd had to say:

I was working the timber northeast of Kloochman Rock on the western edge of the Queets River. I had hiked in about four miles from the Queets ranger station and was set up against a tall pine near the edge of what appeared to be a well-used game trail. Being unfamiliar with the location and after about two hours of seeing nothing, I decided to back track to an area I had passed through on my hike in that looked pretty good, and once again, positioned myself with my back against a large fir. I don't think that I was sitting there for more than ten minutes when I shifted my body to get more comfortable, and something jabbed me right in the ass. I stood up and looked down at the ground, moving some of the mulch and crap out of the way, in order to see what I had sat on. I immediately started to uncover what appeared to me to be human metacarpal or metatarsal bones. In other words, these were the bones from either a human's hand or foot.

I was convinced they were human and not animal, having sat through many hours of skeletal anatomy classes, but what they were doing here by this tree was anyone's guess. I set my gun against the tree and, grabbing a branch, I started to clear away more of the debris on the ground surrounding the base of this large fir. As I did so, I uncovered more bones which I was now certain were the ulnar, radius and humerus bones from a human arm. This now told me that the bones I had first found, were in fact the metacarpal and phalanges from the same arm. I was alone, and I distinctly remember a raw chill going through my entire body, as I realized what I was uncovering.

Having been there, I can speak in all honesty that there is something really eerie about standing in the spot where an unburied human had met their apparent demise, and yet there I found myself alone, deep in the woods. I had actually cleared a decent sized little area with the branch to uncover what I had found as far as bones were concerned. And I could not see nor find any more. So there I stood, trying to make some sense out of having found partial human remains next to the tree. It was then that I started thinking as anyone would have, *just how is it that a human arm and nothing else found its way into the woods detached from its owner?* I remember standing there, rubbing my forehead with my fingers as I was trying to make some sense of it all, when something told me to look up and I did. The initial set of substantial boughs on this large tree, actually began protruding from the trunk some thirty feet or so from the ground.

As I looked up my eyes were immediately drawn to some colored fabric draped across one of the boughs. I could now see enough to realize that I was looking at the remains of a clothed human being laying across this large bough. It was directly above where I had found the bones of the hand and arm. I immediately took note of the fact that there was no tree stand or climbing apparatus attached to the trunk, nor were there smaller limbs that a man or anything else could have supported themselves on to climb this tree to that height. This person had either shimmied up the tree and died, or something else had done the same carrying it up there.

There was no backpack or weapon of any sort visible on the ground surrounding the tree. No sooner had I come to grips with what was already turning out to be a gore fest, that my eyes caught a glimpse of some other colored fabric in a different part of the tree that was also very high off the ground. I walked around the base of the tree to better position myself in order to see whatever it was more clearly. I realized that not only was I seeing the remains of yet another human being, but there was also what appeared to be the carcass of a deer or elk some ten feet away from it, also laying across some boughs. It was at that precise moment in time that I was suddenly keenly aware, deep inside of my innermost being, that I was now being watched. There is no other way of my explaining it to you. I felt as though whoever or whatever had done this terrible deed was now aware that I knew it too, and it, or they, were not happy about it.

I had a long hike out, and although I hadn't planned to leave at this part of the day before I had come upon all of this grizzly stuff, I knew that I had to leave and leave now. That's the way I felt at that moment in time. I suddenly felt as though I was now in imminent danger by remaining here and, quite possibly, on my way out as well.

As I began to make my way out, I must inform you that there were many areas of this forest where something could easily get the jump on you, if it wanted to, and there would be little if any time for you to react. That's just the nature of hunting. We are stalking something in the surroundings in which we ourselves could easily become the hunted if the tables were turned. Today, I was starting to feel as though they had been.

It must have been a mile or so into my outbound hike when I came into what I will call a shallow valley between two hills. I was retracing the way I had come in earlier in the day. The central path between these two hills was damp and soggy to walk on. I could see my boot tracks from earlier in the day, when unexpectedly there, before my eyes, mixed in with my own tracks, were the giant imprints of a human-type foot that were made in the same direction as mine were coming in.

There were about eight of them and many others alongside of the softer muddied area that I could see. I now knew that either a Bigfoot had followed me in or had traversed the same route that I had sometime after me. In either case, it could easily see my tracks and where I was heading. These tracks, although I didn't stop to measure them, were all of twenty to twenty five inches long and in the softer area they were all of six inches into the ground whereas my own were maybe an inch. At that moment, the thought had entered my mind, that I was going to die in the woods that day, and nobody would ever find me. I was hunting with my lever action Winchester that day and I chambered a round.

I had stepped up my pace while being as cautious as I possibly could, taking into consideration the way that I felt at the time. When

I found myself passing through a really dense grouping of trees, I was only about thirty yards, if that, into this grouping when I heard a loud snap that was followed by a deep growl to my right. What happened next was the result of a knee jerk reaction, based entirely on a building fear within me. I turned with my Winchester and emptied it in a fan pattern, quickly ratcheting off every round. I distinctly remember salvo number four, because no sooner had I squeezed it off, than a scream of demonic proportions erupted from the trees. I thought I had shot the devil himself and the screaming didn't stop. I quickly loaded the gun and repeated the same spray pattern that I had just done, firing off six more rounds and started to run faster than I had ever run in my life. I was running and shoving more rounds into the breach as best as I could. The last thing I wanted to do was to turn an ankle or worse, and I could hear this thing wailing behind me, having evidently been shot by round number four.

I covered the last four miles out to the ranger station, faster than I would have believed I could ever run in my lifetime. When I reached the station, the ranger asked me if that was me firing a little while ago up to the north, to which I lied and said no, but that I had heard the shots also. I don't know why, but I didn't want to get into the whole Bigfoot thing and have to explain to him what had happened. I did, however, tell him about what I found in the tree and he was all ears.

Well, the next day, I lead a group of ten lawmen, on foot, back to the location and everyone was as shocked as I was when I first found the bodies. I told the men that I really didn't want to be there anymore, and two of them brought me back out. There was some of the usual questioning, as you can imagine, but I think it was obvious to everyone that I hadn't killed these people or put them up in the tree, either. I am sure that I shot a Bigfoot that day, but I have no tangible proof other than what I have already told you up to this point in time. Who these people were I have no idea, and neither did I follow up at all with law enforcement to ask any further questions regarding this whole grizzly matter, but I will end saying this much. No cougar or any other animal is capable of scaling a bare tree trunk to such heights, carrying a human body out onto a limb and, on top of that, coming back to the same tree several times over and over again. This act had been performed by the Bigfoot and nothing less.

Well, my dear readers, this brings an entirely new meaning to deco-rating a tree. Be very careful in the woods, out there!

The Katahdin Bigfoot Attack

This account was told to me by Cheryl Lamb, whose husband, Charles, had passed away some ten years ago. Here is what Cheryl had to say about her and Charles' sighting:

My husband and I had, for many years, made Maine our go to spot for summer getaways. This whole attraction for Maine had begun after the two of us shared a read of Henry David Thoreau's book, *The Maine Woods*. This was actually our sixth summer vacation in the state. We were camping and canoeing in Katahdin Woods and Waters. I remember the day of the incident as if it was yesterday, being August 27, 1971. The two of us, having risen early from our night's slumber, had prepared a campfire breakfast and afterwards, slipped our canoe into the lake for a morning paddle.

There was a heavy mist floating on the lake that morning. The sun had not yet risen enough to burn it off as we began our paddle slowly following the contour of the lakes eastern shoreline. The lake's appearance was like that of a mirror with the trees along its edge reflecting on its surface. As we were paddling and approaching one of the many bends on the lake's shore, we rounded it to see a cow moose standing ankle deep in the water at lake's edge. She was about a hundred yards away from us as she slowly lifted and turned her head to view the intruders. Moments later, sensing no apparent threat from us, she lowered her head into the lake and began to eat some submerged vegetation. She was standing in the reflection and shade of the trees along the shore, as we watched her for maybe twenty or more minutes.

At some point, Charles whispered to me that he saw something black moving in the brush maybe fifty feet behind the cow, and now both of us had our eyes fixed on the bank. We were seeing what appeared to be a lump of black fur, occasionally protruding from over the top of the brush, and edging closer to where the cow was in the water, yet she was totally unmoved by what we were seeing. Apparently unaware of what was moving closer behind her. What happened next was astounding, to say the least. A creature of incredible proportions leapt out of the brush and, with two large strides, was on the cow, smashing her down headlong into the shallows. She had barely turned her head when the beast prevailed upon her. The beast, which we now realized was a Bigfoot, had driven her head into the lake bottom with her legs kicking and moving briefly as death took hold of her.

The Bigfoot, up until that point in time, was unaware of our presence on the lake. Shortly after the kill, it stood up, rising to its feet and turning to look directly at us. The water in which we sat was only about two feet deep and the spot in which the beast stood, the water level was more than likely less than a foot. I know Charles was thinking exactly what I was. In these shallows that creature could have run us down in a matter of seconds, and done us in as it had with the moose. The two of us immediately started to redirect the canoe to paddle out into deeper water as fast as we could.

The Bigfoot stood its ground, staring us down as we made our way out into the lake. As we paddled quickly to a point where we were now in deep water, perhaps several hundred yards away from the creature, we felt safe enough to stop and watch. It was at this point that the Bigfoot grabbed the cow around the neck, in somewhat of a choke hold, and dragged her carcass out of the lake and into the trees. As you could well imagine, the two of us, having seen this attack take place in such a violent fashion, were in a complete and utter state of shock. It was akin to having a bomb explode in the middle of the night as you slept. The brush on the bank was maybe three or four feet tall and this creature had to have been crawling through it, in order to get close enough to the cow to launch its attack. The speed with which it was able to close the gap from the bank to the moose was incredible.

The Bigfoot must have covered forty or fifty feet in just a few leaps. As it landed on the moose's back, it was visibly at least a couple of feet taller than the moose's height, even in its hunched position on the moose's body. When it stood over the moose and turned its gaze towards us, it had to have been all of eight or nine feet tall and as big as a house. Standing defiantly and facing us, its arms hung out and away from its body, apparently forced to do so because of the size and dimensions of its musculature.

As it stood in the misty shadows, the Bigfoot's fur appeared to be almost black in color and virtually covered its entire body. The other incredible aspect of this event, was the apparent ease with which the beast was able to carry away its kill. I have no idea how much this moose weighed. But it was at least as big as a large horse and the Bigfoot wrapped its arm around its neck and casually walked away with it into the trees. It didn't struggle with it or drag it so much as a foot. It simply picked it up and walked away like it was nothing at all. We didn't see any blows thrown by the beast either. It seemed to just drive the cows head into the lake bottom in somewhat of a choke hold, and it was all over and done with rather quickly.

The Desolation Peak Sighting

This account was told to me by Perry Michaels, a resident of Washington State. Here is what Perry had to say about his sighting that July day:

I was with a group of seven hikers, all of whom were, and are, personal friends of mine. All of us regularly hike together. We were walking in a line, spaced maybe some ten or fifteen feet apart, at a fairly high elevation nearing our destination of Desolation Peak. We were on a fairly steep slope that was in bloom with thousands of wildflowers, with Ross Lake in view, far below us in the distance. The slope that we were on descends to form what I will refer to as a valley between it and an adjoining hillside off to our left. Aside from the grass and the wildflowers, which give this area the appearance of an alpine meadow in Europe, everywhere that you looked there were clusters of what I believe are small spruce trees; none of which, I believe, are more than twenty five to thirty feet tall. Many of them seem much smaller than that.

The day was beautiful, with the exception of a haze that was hanging over both the mountain and the lake below us. The haze in no way hindered our ability to see very far in virtually any direction. This entire area is covered in thirty percent trees and the rest is all open meadow-like terrain, which is covered in grass and flowers. The reason I mention all of this is so that you understand, that unless something or someone was to deliberately stop to conceal itself in a patch of small trees, it would only be a matter of moments before it would be visible again as it walked.

Whenever we as a group get together, there is very little chatter going on amongst us, because we are all of the same kindred spirit. We hike to get away and immerse ourselves in the natural world, and part of that escape is to leave jabbering behind. We were about four hours into the hike having reached the area that I just described to you, when Joey, who was taking the lead, had stopped and pointed towards the base of the adjoining slope saying, "Hey guys, check that out."

From our position, we were more than likely a thousand feet higher, looking down across this valley at two figures walking in single file below us on the opposing slope. These two figures were both very dark in color from head to toe, and were walking on two legs, with what I will describe as a rather unusual type of gait.

Both Joey and I were carrying good field glasses. The two of us brought both of the creatures into focus, immediately realizing that what we were looking at were two Sasquatch. Talking quietly, everyone wanted to have a look at the critters, so we passed the glasses back and forth amongst us, watching the creatures walk along the slope. With the exception of them passing from time to time behind some of these short trees that I described to you earlier, we watched them walk for well over a thousand yards or more. It was at that point when the pair of creatures entered into a small patch of trees, but did not come out on the other side.

At that moment, we collectively decided to descend the slope, keeping ourselves well concealed as we did so, in hopes of getting a closer look at them when they reemerged from the cover of the trees. Having descended the slope angling ourselves towards where we knew they were, we had now achieved a distance of maybe 500 yards away from them and we dared not get any closer. It's not that we were afraid so to speak, but the slope from this point forward was virtually devoid of any further tree cover on our side. Each of us sat hidden behind a number of trees, waiting and hoping that the Sasquatch would once again show themselves. Our group sat still and watched this patch of trees intently for the better part of an hour, when one of the Sasquatch came darting out of the trees. It was in pursuit of what we could see was some type of small critter running around on the ground.

Speaking for myself at the time, I thought it was a groundhog or something of the sort. After a brief pursuit, it looked to me like the creature stomped on it and killed it. I say this because it stopped running suddenly and I couldn't see the critter running anymore either. With that, the creature reached down to the ground and lifted something into the air, which to my eyes was a dead animal. With that, it reentered the cover of the trees and some ten minutes later, both of them came back into view. I put my glasses on them squarely and could see that they were both holding at least several of the same type of animal in their hands.

Initially, as we waited, we were all wondering what they were doing in this patch of trees for an hour. However, now we knew they had gone in there for a reason. There was obviously some type of den or burrow in there where they acquired these animals. Perhaps they were waiting at the entrance or even digging it up, which is something we will never know. What we do know is what we saw. They had come empty handed and were leaving with both hands full. The two of them casually began to retrace their steps back in the direction from where we had first seen them. Using the average tree height around us as a gauge, I estimated that they were somewhere between eight and twelve feet tall. Of course, we had no way of really telling, but they were certainly very tall and broad. At one point as they were walking, the one taking up the rear actually kind of swatted the one in front with one of the dead critters on its back.

To me, it looked very much like a gesture of kidding around, like you or I would do with each other. The entire sighting was obviously something that none of us would ever forget. I have to say that up until that point in my life, I hadn't really given their existence much thought. Having seen the pictures and heard the stories, it was more or less a meaningless thing to me as to whether or not they did or didn't exist. After that day, my viewpoint and outlook has obviously changed dramatically. These creatures are in fact real and now the seven of us know it for ourselves.

The Twin Tree Lake Sighting

This sighting was brought to my attention by Roger Waters, who was doing a little group trail riding in 1968 within Jasper Park, Canada. For those of you who have read, Bigfoot: Terror in the Woods, Volume One, *you will recall a couple of hikers who had an encounter in this same region with a Bigfoot foraging on a log. Here is what Roger had to say (this is not, by the way, Roger Waters of rock and roll fame):*

We had arranged to go on a group horseback and camping expedition up near the Canadian Rockies in 1968. It's so long ago, that I don't remember the exact name, but it was an extraordinary location and wilderness experience. At the time, we were heading out for I believe three or four days. However, at eighty-nine, my memory is not quite as sharp as it used to be. This is a fact that you will understand only when you get there, my friend. We had just got through our first overnighter and were well into the second day when we came to a place called the Outlet of Twin Tree Lake.

This was, as I recall, a shallow stream that was flanked heavily by dense spruce or pines of some sort. Perhaps they were firs, but I just don't remember. As we approached this body of water, both of its banks were fairly wide and covered in what I will call gravel. They were not large boulders, but actual glacial gravel that we and the horses could walk on without fear of being injured. We had all dismounted from our horses and were holding them by the reins while they took a rest and drank from the stream. From our vantage point, the stream took a bend to the left some two hundred yards away from our position, which was concealed by the trees hugging the banks for as far as we could see. Beyond this bend and the trees, the Rockies were visible in the distance; an absolutely breathtaking sight to behold.

The horses had only been drinking for ten minutes or so when a couple of them started getting a little restless. This restlessness quickly escalated into an all-out panic within about thirty seconds from the start. While trying to control her horse, one of the women was kicked in the wrist, rendering her wrist broken. She let go of her horse and it ran off. In the midst of this sudden melee, the guide was now trying to hold his horse while also trying to tend to the injured woman.

All of us really had our hands full, as you would well imagine. I should add that only a couple of people in the group were avid riders. While we were all trying to come to grips with what exactly was going on, with most of us being very inexperienced in the skills of a true horseman, one of the members shouted out, "What the hell is that?" As we all tried to gain control of our horses, we were now also looking upstream where he was looking, and saw a large black two legged creature, standing on the gravel bank a hundred yards away from where we were.

Its appearance was that of a tremendous and tall gorilla, completely covered in fur from head to toe. This gorilla was standing on the bank watching the commotion as it rocked back and forth looking directly at us. Now we knew that apparently the horses had noticed it before we had, and were none too happy about its presence. The guide, looking at the gorilla, starting shouting directly at it, "Go, bear!" He repeated it several times in succession, which seemed to work because, only moments later, the creature retreated back into the trees never to be seen again.

A few minutes after the gorilla had left, the horses finally calmed down. The woman's wrist that had gotten kicked was either broken or very badly bruised, which meant, at any rate, that we would be heading back sooner than previously anticipated. The guide mounted up and went to retrieve the runaway horse, which by the way, we could see, was not that far away from our location. Upon the guide's return, we all helped the injured woman get back onto the guide's horse; the two of them now riding together. Her horse was then tethered to one of the other's for the long ride out. Thankfully, this whole thing had gone down fairly early in the day. Once were we reorganized, we actually made it all the way back out only spending maybe the last hour of the day under partial darkness. Our main concern was getting the woman to medical attention as soon as possible.

Nevertheless, on the return ride we were all talking about what it was that we had seen. Some were saying it was a monster, while I had called it a gorilla, not knowing what to really make of it. The guide said that he had used the term *bear* while shouting at it because he didn't know what to say. Some were saying it was a giant, hairy, Neanderthal man. I now know that what we saw that day was a Bigfoot, but at the time, I also thought it was a monster of some sort. This thing was gigantic and even at a distance, I could see that its chest was in a distinct V-shape, like that of a muscle man. When it turned to retreat into the woods, it only took two steps to disappear, which may have been more than fifteen feet in my estimation. I'll be honest with you having seen it with my own two eyes, I was glad to get out of there alive and in one piece.

Saved by the Roar

This account was told to me by Max Schein, who was referencing a trip he and his wife had taken to Grand Teton National Park. Here is what Max had to say about their encounter:

Well, Bill, it's like I told you earlier, that my wife and I, along with another couple who live near to us, had made our way into the park and were staying at the lodge near Jenny Lake. Mind you, I am sixty-seven years old now, but at the time, all of us were in our thirties or early forties. We had planned to take a day hike within the vicinity of Moran Canyon. Afterwards, we would take a break near the southwest corner of Jackson Lake.

We had made our way north around the shore of Leigh Lake and had passed between Trapper and Bearpaw Lakes. We were heading north, approaching Jackson Lake and the entrance to Moran Canyon. As we were entered the canyon, Bivouac Peak was to the north (on our right hand side) and Mount Moran was just to the south (on our left side). Both of these mountains are in excess of eleven thousand feet, and create quite a grand entrance to the canyon.

As we found ourselves well into the canyon, we were well immersed in some very dense foliage on both sides of the trail. Our visibility was extremely limited, unable to see what, if anything, may be lurking alongside of us as we walked. It must have been about twenty minutes walking into the canyon when my friend, John, said that he heard something just ahead of us and off to our right. "Thank God," is all that I can say for someone who has better hearing than me! I say this because no more than thirty seconds after he had said that and we had paused to listen, a huge grizzly came walking into the path just ahead of us.

If we hadn't paused, we would have walked directly alongside of him. The bear stopped and stood on his hind legs, looking directly at us, and let out a fierce growl. John immediately stepped forward and was now shoulder to shoulder with me with our wives behind us, clutching at our clothes. The two of us both grabbed our bear sprays and stood at the ready. This monster was now standing, some nine or ten feet tall, and was less than fifty feet away, looking directly at us. His stare reminded me of looking at the blank eyes of a shark that has, nor shows, any mercy towards its victim. My heart was trembling within me. I would be lying to you if I said anything less than I thought someone, or everyone, was going to die that day. We started to back up very slowly, which may or may not have been a big mistake. As we did, the bear lowered itself to the ground and started to slowly creep towards us, swinging its head back and forth.

John and I both had the cans pointed directly at him, preparing for the worst, when the craziest and most unexpected thing occurred. A bizarre, shrieking sound of the loudest volume that you can imagine, erupted in the canyon, the sound of which I thought would shatter my ear drums. Our wives screamed and the bear flung its head to its right in response to this shriek. I couldn't pinpoint the direction of the howl, but the bear seemed to be able to sense exactly the direction from which the sound had come. No sooner had he turned to his right, he bolted off the side of the trail into the brush, never to be seen again.

The shrieking was so loud and deep, that I could actually feel the vibrations passing through my very being. The volume and intensity of it was much too high for it to have been created at a distance. Whatever this was that had roared, it was obvious to us that the enormous grizzly bear wanted nothing to do with it. I remember that I was breathing heavily and had thought for a moment that I may have been having a heart attack. We all looked at each other, and both of our wives were in tears, trembling in fear. We decided to get while the getting was good, and started to move back out of the canyon and quickly. I think it was about ten minutes into what I will refer to as "our escape," that John, once again, heard something on our flank that seemed to be pacing us.

All I could think of was that the bear had come back for its meal. We were all terrified. John was at the front and I was taking up the rear as we moved, as quickly as we could, out of the canyon. It seemed like hours had passed, but at some point, we broke out into a more open area where we were no longer surrounded by bushes. We could now see in every direction and there was, at least for now, nothing pursuing us.

Late that afternoon, we had made it back to the lodge and had sat down as a group for drinks and some food. As we rehashed yet again what had happened in the canyon, it was John's wife, Debbie, who first breached the subject of Sasquatch at the table. We had heard the grizzly growl at close range. Even if it had intensified, it could never have reached the decibel level of what we had heard. She was correct in saying this, for what else were we to say? If it was a Sasquatch, it may have very well saved us from harm or even death. It very well may have actually followed us out until we were safe. There is really nothing more than I can tell you other than that which I have already said. We were so afraid in the presence of this grizzly, that I cannot even begin to imagine how we would have felt if it was the Sasquatch standing there in front of us instead.

The Great Smoky Sighting

This account was told to me by Nicholas Obratsov, a resident of the great state of Tennessee and a transplant from the old Soviet Union. He is a physicist, and was quite the skeptic until the day of his own encounter, an encounter of which you shall soon hear. This is what Nicholas had to share:

My good friend, named Hector Jimenez, just happens to be the landscaper at my home. Some might say, "How is it that a physicist befriends a laborer?" I will answer that question quite succinctly. Over time, in conversing with Hector at my home, I found that he had great interest not only in all things plant related around the house, but with everything found in the forest, as well. He, having no formal education whatsoever, other than what he had self-taught himself in the course of being a landscaper, had given me more than a run for my money through the years, with the wealth of knowledge that he possessed in regards to all things botanical. Having had many invaluable conversations with him over time, and knowing him to be as fit as a fiddle, at some point, the two of us became engaged in regular forest hikes together, as a somewhat leisurely activity and a form of staying fit. And so, the bond of landscaper and physicist was formed. Over a period of about fifteen years, Hector and I have been through just about every square mile of the Great Smoky National Park and the Nantahala National Forest. I would be willing to wager, if it could be proven, that the two of us have hiked a hundred thousand miles together, between the two wildernesses.

In the summer of 2015, we had made our way over to the Clingmans Dome observation tower. From there, we were scoping out some promising areas in the region of the Little Rivers tributaries. The following weekend, we hiked into the area coming from the Newfound Gap Road in the area of the Chimney Tops and immediately found ourselves in the midst of an extremely rigorous hike through the timber. Our plan for the day was to hike in until we hit water and then to follow what we had found until we ran out of time. Our typical day hike involves allowing ourselves enough time to get in and out of where we are, including the possibility of one of us turning an ankle or the like, which has actually happened. You don't want to be stuck in the forest at night.

We were about three hours in, when we heard a tremendous crash of a tree falling to the ground to our southwest. After hearing it, we decided to alter our plan to that of finding the tree that had fallen, so we commenced to hike in that direction. We had walked about another mile when we heard yet a second tree come crashing down, followed by what sounded like a loud conversation in a foreign dialect. Now, you know, Bill, that I am from Russia. To me, it sounded like one of the Siberian dialects of which I do not speak, nor do I understand.

Hector and I, being uncertain as to just what we may be walking into, started to move much more slowly and yet, nevertheless, stayed the course to find those who were talking. After stalking for what must have been another hundred yards, this jabbering conversation was getting ever louder. Suddenly, we saw a huge, black creature moving just ahead, and the two of us simultaneously dropped to our knees behind some bushes. The beast had walked behind maybe six or seven trees and seemed to be talking as it did so. Then, as quickly as it had appeared, it had moved out of our sight.

We were astonished at what we had just seen. It was unmistakably a large, bipedal giant covered in brown fur and the size of an ox. I can tell you that it was all of four meters tall and better than a meter in thickness, at the very least. It had the physique of a massive body builder, and we had no desire to learn how they were felling trees. For fear of our very lives, Hector and I immediately started to retreat, not knowing how we would be greeted should we be found out by this beast and its cohort.

As we backtracked, we could hear two very distinct voices, one being higher pitched than the other in its tone. They were making so much noise between the speech and the rustling of the timbers, that we had no fear of being heard as we retreated from our position. It was obvious to us that they were not expecting any company in these woods and were doing nothing to quiet themselves in any way. Some may say, "Why didn't you stay to see more and to listen to them?"

To which, I would retort, "Unless you wanted to die, there would be no reason to stay." We were so frightened by the very site of one monster that we did not need to see a second. All we wanted to do was get away, and quickly.

In Russia, we have a saying similar to that which I have heard in this country, that being, "I will believe it when I see it." Well, that day I had moved from being skeptical about the creature known as Bigfoot, to being a full on believer, having now seen one with my very own eyes. Besides the actual sighting, the most amazing aspect was that of the spoken language between them. There was a distinct back and forth, like two old washwomen, going on between them the entire time we were near to them. To date, it was the most incredible event of my lifetime.

The Empty Tent Affair

This rather chilling testimonial came to me by way of Andy Chern-off, a resident of British Columbia. If nothing that I have written has blown your mind up until this point, hold on to your hat because it is about to get a little rough.

Well you know, Bill, in preparation for this interview, I had many things that were passing through my mind as far as what I was going to say is concerned. I decided for some strange reason to bring you way back into my teenage years where this lifestyle of mine actually began, in the hope that it will help somebody else out there who may be a lot like me. It will also help to clarify why I was where I was when this whole affair came to be.

As a young man I had a troubled upbringing, to say the least. The home in which I lived was not exactly a loving and kind environment to grow up in. I think I was about fourteen or fifteen years old, when I made the acquaintance of a beautiful and cheery girl around the corner from me. It was love at first sight. She had a beautiful sister who was slightly older than her and their family was everything that mine was not. As the next couple of years progressed, there wasn't anything that I wanted to do more than to hang out with her and hold her hand. There is much more than I have time to say or care to say, but after about two years and out of the clear blue sky, she broke up with me and the tears flowed like water.

For the rest of my life, I was truly unable to fall in love again. Although I had some friends and relationships, nothing was ever the same. After many years had passed, someone met her at a high school reunion and overheard her say, "I should have married Andy." Upon my hearing of that, the wound was reopened, and badly. Through the many years, as they passed, I had become as the song title so aptly said, "The Solitary Man." I didn't necessarily like to be alone, but found myself in that state more often than not, especially when it came to hunting and fishing. My married friends just don't have the same freedom or zeal to do the things that I do, and so it is that I am predominantly solo.

During my relationship with this girl, she had given me, on my birthday, a necklace. It was of the head of Christ, overlaid on a cross, and it had both of our names etched into the back. Many years after the breakup, I took the necklace out of my dresser drawer and threw it into the sea, never to be seen again. Well, as fate would have it, a seed had been planted in my life, and as time passed, I had entered into a new love affair with Jesus Christ. It was this love affair that fulfilled all the things in my life that had been lost and then some.

In August of 2001, I planned to backpack into the Banff for the weekend in the hope of finding some new and suitable hunting grounds for the fall. I was somewhere in the area of Mount Rich-ardson and the Pipestone River at the time. During the course of the first day, the majority of my time was spent just getting up to and into the area that I had in mind, with only a couple of hours left in the day to do a little reconnaissance, if you will, of the area. The following morning, having spent the night in my bag by the fire, I arose to a beautiful new morning and started hiking due northeast into an area that I hadn't been in before. I was coming over a low lying ridge that was looking down into somewhat of a hollow, when I noticed what I believed was a tent in the trees below my position. I decided to go down and introduce myself to whoever was there.

It took me maybe ten minutes to make it to the tent. When I final-ly walked up on it, the tent was half knocked down and the campsite appeared to have been abandoned. The aluminum poles on the one side were collapsed and I could see a large clean cut in the fabric of the tent on the same side as the collapsed poles. For whatever rea-son, I took a moment to lift the poles back into place, straightening them in the process, in order to get the tent back into form. Having done so, I walked around to the front, where the entry flap had been torn open, and I stuck my head inside.

Lying on the floor of the tent was the fully dressed corpse of a man in what was a pool of dried up blood that covered most of the tents floor. There was a handgun lying on the floor and numerous expended shell casings were strewn about. A chill came over my body that is indescribable. It wasn't all about what I was seeing, but all I can say is that I felt like I was now being watched by whoever had done this hideous deed. My hair was standing on end and I was trembling. There were three sleeping bags in the tent and two were stained in blood, and yet there was only one man. The stench gagged me as I looked more closely at him, so I pressed my handkerchief against my nose and mouth.

The flesh was all but gone from the bones, and yet there was something odd about the body as I stood over it looking down. The entire ribcage seemed to be collapsed to within a few inches of the ground. His chest looked like a balloon that had the air let out of it. The clothes were basically flat to the tent's floor. I shuddered and turned my gaze to the torn tent wall. What I had seen on the outside as a cut to the side of the tent looked like it may have been made from the inside as a means of escape, but from what? Or who?

I must tell you that at this point in time, I was in a state of shock. I continued to survey the inside and now took note of the fact that there were some large footprints on the tent's floor that were made of dried blood. It was difficult to say how many because they were all overlapping each other and smeared around. There was one that I could see clearly and it consisted of the toes, heel, and ball of a giant foot. It was like a man's, only shaped very oddly. It was then that I stepped back outside and started to look around in the direction that someone may have went, had the person fled through the torn side of the tent. I walked about thirty feet from the tent where I came upon a buck knife lying open on the ground.

As I began to scan around the knife, there it was: another body, fully clothed and lying face up on the ground. Walking over to the corpse, I looked down on the body and I was struggling to keep my composure. I say this because he only appeared to be face up. What I was actually looking at was a dead man, lying face down, whose head had been twisted around, facing now backwards. I could see the neck bones and they were completely disconnected from each other.

I went back over by the tent to confirm in my mind that I had seen three sleeping bags and I had. Where was the third person? I continued to look around. The feeling of being watched was now amplified within me. I looked around for about another hour or so and could not find a third person. God only knows what happened to that individual in the woods.

I returned to the body lying on the ground and took the wallet out of the back pants pocket. As I took the driver's license out, I was looking at the smiling face of a twenty seven year old man named Walter, who was now a decaying mass of bones laying in the woods. I began to weep profusely. A great sadness fell over me as my mind tried to comprehend the scene which I was standing in as it must have occurred. The footprints could only have been those of a Sasquatch. The man whose body was on the floor of the tent had obviously fired numerous rounds in an effort to fight off the invader and had lost. When I went back into the tent, I saw four shell casings; perhaps there were more that I hadn't seen.

The sheer terror that must have unfolded in this campsite was enveloping me as I stood there. One thing that struck me was that the bodies had not been torn apart by anything else in the woods, for they were completely intact as they had met their death. I left this place hiking double time until I had made it fully back to my vehicle, which was nothing less than a ten hour speed hike. I didn't know I had it in me, but I couldn't stop to rest. The entire time I was in fear of my life and that kept me going full tilt.

Well, my dear readers, a body with its chest caved in and man with his head spun around backwards. Pools of dried blood and empty shell casings. It really makes you want to wander around in the dark

with a night vision scope, unarmed, looking for Bigfoot, doesn't it...
or does it?

The Congaree Crowler

This account was made known to me by Tommy Nelson and his wife, Charlotte, a couple who, at the time of this sighting, were residents in the state of South Carolina. Here is what they had to say about their encounter:

I must begin by telling you, Bill, that the absolute furthest thing from myself and my wife's minds at the time of this sighting was a Bigfoot encounter. I don't believe we had even spoken about the term *Bigfoot* so much as once in the seventeen years, at the time, that we had been together. I am retired now, but in the late nineties when this whole thing went down, I was a regional director for a major retail franchise in the United States. My position was inclusive of many moves around the states and overseeing the successful building and startup of the new franchise locations.

With that in mind, in 1998, we were living in South Carolina for a period of about eighteen months. The two of us spent a fair amount of time hiking and renting canoes and boats wherever we found ourselves. We had no real long term friendships, so for the most part, it was me and Charlotte doing whatever we needed to do to entertain ourselves and stay in shape. It was on my birthday that year, September 30, which we were going back into the Congaree National Park to do some exploring and burn up some calories. The last time we were in the park, we had been canoeing on Cedar Creek, so for a change, we had decided to take a good, long hike to see what another area of the park had to offer.

Congaree National Park has a very unique and diverse ecosystem. It is comprised of some 24,000 acres and is the largest old growth bottomland hardwood forest in the country remaining. The park itself is a also a floodplain, which means that the park is relatively drier or damp, based on Mother Nature's activities, as it relates to the Congaree River (which is the southern border of the park itself). As a result, there are many creeks and bogs, creating habitats for lots of nasty snakes, otters, lizards and all kinds of other wildlife within and around the park's boundaries. Due to its diversity, the park often serves as a research site for the scientific community.

Our itinerary was to hike the Kingsnake, Oak Ridge River, and the Weston Lake Trails, which are all interconnected, and would bring us back to where we had started from. Charlotte and I had made our way well past what I would call the half way point in the hike, and we were making our way back to an area called The Gut, where, eventually, we would meet up with the Weston Lake Trail. We were casually hiking along, when my wife grabbed me by the arm and said, "Tommy, look over there by that big tree. I just saw something."

Now, the area she was pointing at consisted of bald cypress trees, some of which are quite massive in their girth. Many of them sit proud on the earth with a fair amount of root exposed, making them even wider at their base. I said to her, "Which tree are you talking about?" She pointed, saying, "That one over there with the other big one right in front of it."

Looking into the woods, there were two exceptionally large, cypress trees, with one being some twenty feet behind the other. From our perspective, they appeared to be side by side, if you took your depth perception out of the equation. Between the two of them, they were consuming about seven feet of width in our field of view. My wife said to me, "I saw something big duck behind that tree in the rear."

We stood there, very still, for a few moments and then started to move forward a few steps to see if we could look behind them, so to speak. I think we had moved maybe five or six steps when this tremendous creature, which we now realized was a Bigfoot, darted out from behind the tree and ran into the surrounding forest and undergrowth. The entire episode was over from start to finish in a matter of seconds.

The two of us nearly jumped out of our skin when this Bigfoot bolted. The speed and ease with which it ran away from us was just incredible. Neither one of us had seen its face. My wife later recounted that she had only seen its dark fur out of the corner of her eye, when it was almost completely behind the cypress, and had no idea that this was what would pop out. When it took off, there was virtually no sound that could be heard. In this area, the ground was probably moister than some of the other areas of the park, but still it ran away like a whisper. It had to have covered some seventy five yards or more before we lost sight of it.

My wife and I walked over by the tree it had been standing behind. We could see some impressions in the ground, but nothing that I would venture to call a footprint. The ground and grass were simply crushed and matted down. There was a tiny, scraggly-looking branch hanging off from the side of the tree in front, which we were able to use to gauge its height. When it ran away, I could see all of its head just below that little branch. Having walked over to and now standing under the branch, I extended my arm straight up to try and touch it, but it was out of reach. At the time, I didn't know the distance between my hand and the branch.

When we came home, I did the same thing in our apartment, reaching my hand towards the ceiling and using the distance between the two as a reference. Upon doing this, I realized that the Bigfoot was about nine feet tall or better. I did mention that, between the two trees, they were blocking about seven feet of our view, which was why we couldn't see the Bigfoot. When it had committed itself to fleeing, it was all of five to six feet wide at the shoulders and cut like a seasoned gymnast; so massive were its shoulder muscles that, from the rear, we could only see what appeared to be the top of its head as it ran away.

My wife and I had a long conversation after the sighting which revolved around the old "what if" scenario. We were both in total agreement that the way the Bigfoot moved and ran with such stealth, that if it wanted to, it could run up on you or anything else and snatch you before you knew what hit you. My own opinion is that because of the creature's enormous weight, coupled with the gigantic feet that it possesses, it simply compresses the crunch, if you will, out of whatever it steps on; thereby, muffling the sound from our ears. I have no other explanation other than that, knowing that when my wife and I walked over by the same trees, we made noise and the Bigfoot didn't.

The hair on it looked like it was a dark, rusty brown color with some threads of grey mixed in. Having said that, nothing about its movements indicated this was, by any means, an old man, so to speak. It was extremely agile and fast as it made its exit. We weren't afraid other than when it first made its move. I don't think that I would say the same if the move it made had been in our direction. That would have been an entirely different story and quite probably one that I may not be alive to tell, had it occurred.

The Grouse Meadow Sighting

This sighting was brought to my attention by Dr. Ronaldo Gideon, a man of Haitian origin who is now a U.S. citizen and resident physician. Here is what the good doctor had to share:

Within the hospital where I am employed, there is a small group of us who regularly go to Cross-Fit together. To expand our fitness routine beyond the classes, we began doing a variety of other things together to maintain our physical fitness, including hiking on a routine basis. Several times a year if we are able, some, if not all of our group, try to get together for a weekend hike in a really special location. Such was the case in August of 2015 when this sighting occurred. There were six members of our group that travelled up to Kings Canyon Park in search of some well needed rest from our busy hospital schedules. It was a beautiful Saturday morning and we had begun our ride in the dark of night in order to ensure an early arrival.

The people in our group, if I do say so myself, are in excellent physical condition. For most people if they were to tag along with us for the day, they would think that they had gone jogging rather than hiking. We had made our way well into an area of the park known as Grouse Meadow, where we decided to sit down by a body of water and take a break for some food and drink. From where we sat, we were looking over a small area of water that was surrounded by brown and green grasses which ran a short distance, being interrupted by many stands of what I believe are cedar or spruce trees. The trees then continued for maybe four hundred yards where they began to grow, ascending up the slopes of the mountains that were directly in front of us.

After we were relaxed, I had asked the group to pose in front of this beautiful view for a picture. They stood with their backs to it as I snapped a couple of shots. I then took my place in the lineup, handing off the camera to the respiratory therapist of our little clan named Julius. As Julius stood facing us, just after he had told everyone to smile, he said to all of us, "Hey guys, what the heck is that?"

As he raised his arm pointing over our heads, we all spun around wondering what it was that he was talking about. There was an area of slope running up the side of the mountain's base that was nearest to us, that was fairly devoid of any of tree cover. In this space, you could see for hundreds of yards anything that might be coming down from the mountain or going up to it. Once our eyes were fixed on the slope, we could all see what appeared to be a large, dark figure walking down the side of the slope heading towards the valley below that we ourselves were now standing in.

Several of the members of our group had binoculars and were

quick to put them right on our man, shall we say. The cry from those who were looking first was immediate and resounding: it was a Sasquatch and there was absolutely no doubt about it. The binoculars were all passed to those who hadn't yet seen it and afterward, we were all in one accord as to what it was we were looking at. The fact of the matter is this: the very moment that your eyes see this creature, it is unmistakable and your mind is immediately able to tell you what it is you are looking at.

It's very much in the same light as seeing a frog on a lily pad in the pond. You are not confused when you see it, but rather you know what you are looking at. I and everyone else with me knew in an instant that this was a Sasquatch and not a man in a dark outfit. None of us had ever seen one before and yet, we all knew emphatically what it was. It was covering a tremendous amount of ground and quickly, which a human could not do walking down this same steep slope. To the eye, one could see that the size of its feet were enormous. Its legs seemed to be striding at well over ten feet per step. The other thing that I noticed was that it kept its arms virtually steady and hanging at its sides for the entire descent off the mountain. It was as though it had no fear or notion of falling or slippage.

The arms were another dead giveaway as to what the creature was, as they hung with its fingers surpassing its knees. It had to have descended well over five hundred yards or more in maybe two minutes as we were watching it. After, it reached a point near the base where the trees obscured our view. Some of the members of our group wanted to run forward and try to see it close up, to which I said, "No way." I then followed by saying, "Who knows, it may be coming our way right now." We all stepped behind some cover as we waited to see if it would arrive. It didn't, much to the dismay of some of the group's members.

I, for one, was more than happy and amazed to have seen the Bigfoot at all, especially having done so from a position where nobody was in any imminent danger. Frankly, I wouldn't have believed it had someone else told me about it. I think this is just human nature. To most, this is the stuff of folklore and legend and nothing more. It makes for a good campfire story in the darkness of night. My colleagues back at the hospital were in an uproar when they heard about our sighting; the joke being that maybe one will show up in the E.R. and the like, which was said in good fun. As for myself and the rest of the group that was there that day, Bigfoot is now a reality and walking around in California.

The Moro Rock Sighting

I have taken the liberty of placing this sighting directly after the previous one to prove a point. This sighting had occurred under virtually the same circumstances as the hospital workers in the same month; just a year later. The real kicker is that it happened less than seventy five miles south in Sequoia National Park. I will now step into the background and allow Steven Gonsalves to tell his story.

I wish that I had more to say, Bill, but I am not much of a talker. I kind of just wanted to let someone know who would listen and not be critical of what I and my friend, Willie, had seen that day from Moro Rock. This is actually a regular stop for us, as we love to hike in there and sit on the rock as our midway point.

It was August 14, 2016, that we had hiked in and were up on the rock as is our usual habit. From this point, you are looking at The Great Western Divide in the High Sierra in the distance, which amounts to a lot of enormous snow covered mountains. Going out and away in the direction I was looking, there is somewhat of a valley that is formed by a variety of slopes descending into one area, forming kind of a V-shape in the terrain. On my left side, as I was sitting on the rock, are quite a few pines that continue down the slope for quite some distance. The boughs from these pines somewhat obscure your view of the slopes off to the left of where we sat.

From my position, there was an opening, if you will, in some of the boughs next to me, that otherwise were completely impeding my ability to see. It was out of my peripheral vision that I picked up on something dark moving down a slope off to the left; many hundreds of yards away, but in the open. There are certain slopes which, for whatever reason, are virtually clear of trees and others that are covered almost entirely. This slope in particular had none. I immediately pointed it out to Willie, and we both stood up where we could see clearly what it was we were looking at with our field glasses. Before I could utter a word, Willie said, "It's a damn Bigfoot, man!"

I couldn't have agreed with him more. We were standing there on that rock and looking out over the valley, watching a large, two-legged, tall, black beast walking down the slope towards the valley below.

This creature had no idea it was being observed. At one point, it had actually stopped and started to swing its arms around in a way that made us think it was kind of stretching out. When it stopped, it turned its head, and I swore that it was looking directly at us for maybe ten seconds or more. Then, it casually started walking down the slope again, eventually disappearing into the trees in the valley below.

The two of us high fived each other and were ecstatic about what we had just seen. Not even in our wildest dreams did either of us expect such a thing to happen, and yet it had. My glasses are a hundred power and they are so big that I carry them in my pack. I typically use them for star gazing, but when I fixed them on this critter, I had a bird's eye view of him with great clarity. He was so heavily muscled that it looked like he had large lumps all over his body. You could see the leg muscles pumping outward and shaking his fur as he walked down the hill. You or I would really have to hustle to keep pace with the way this thing was moving and even then, we would more than likely end up falling or breaking an ankle.

Between the two of us, we spend a lot of time in the backcountry. In all the years, we had never seen anything like this. Dozens of bears, elk, deer, wild horses, sheep, and even a cougar, but never did we think that we would be adding a Bigfoot to the list. Now we had.

The Stolen Deer Evidence

The account was told to me by Paul Cataldi, a man now living in New Jersey who spent his youth in western Tennessee. Let's listen in as Paul tells us what happened to him, his uncle, and his father in the fall of 1968:

My dad and uncle used to regularly hunt deer in the western hills during the fall. At the time of this occurrence of which I am about to speak, I was only ten years old and not quite ready to handle a long rifle in the woods. Nevertheless, my dad and uncle took me along for the hunt. My dad and his brother always hunted together, and my dad was the older of the two by six years. On this particular day, I remember that it was quite chilly, and we were set up by the edge of an old farm field. Looking back, I think they had an agreement of some kind with the owner to be there. We had got into the area just before sunup and by seven o'clock, the shot rang out, and my uncle had scored a six pointer.

When I tell people the things that we used to eat on a regular basis, living now in New Jersey, they generally cringe at the very thought of it. Back then, we ate deer, possum, raccoon, rabbit, and damn near anything that you could take down with a gun. I remember my uncle saying that the deer had to go all of two hundred pounds, and it sure was a nice animal. To get it out of the woods, they had to make what is little known today as a *carry pole*. Uncle Joe carried a small hatchet in a belt sheath, and he would cut down a small sapling and trim it up. This would become a carrying pole that they would sling the deer to.

While Uncle Joe was trimming up the tree, my dad had flipped the deer on its side and had begun to tie the four legs together and apply a rope to the antlers. When Uncle Joe was done, he laid the pole next to the deer's feet and head and my dad helped to rope the deer to the pole. With that, they crouched down in the front and rear of the deer and hoisted him up on their shoulders to carry him out of the woods; the deer now being suspended between them on the pole. We had a long walk in and now, we were going to have a longer walk back out carrying the deer, but you never heard a word from my dad or uncle about it being difficult.

As a funny side note, the vehicle that we came in was named, "The Shit Wagon," by Uncle Joe. I always thought it was funny when he said *shit* because my dad never cursed. It was an old Country Squire station wagon that was given to him. He cut the roof out of the back up to the front bench seat and had made a partition wall; sealing off the front from the now open back. This was a poor man's pickup truck that he used to shovel manure into, amongst other things, for his garden. Hence the name The Shit Wagon. We were about halfway back to The Shit Wagon, when my dad said that he wanted to put the deer down and check out another spot for a minute with my uncle and me.

By the way, I should mention that there was absolutely nobody around here. We had driven in on a dirt road, full of bumps and ditches, and had walked hundreds of yards through a trail to get to where we were hunting. If you broke down in here, it was going to be a long day. My dad and uncle laid the deer down gently and we proceeded to walk off into the woods to inspect this area that my dad was talking about.

We had been gone for about fifteen minutes, having inspected what was a nice little meadow back in the trees, and had turned around to head back out of the woods. When we had made it back out to the path, all of us were looking around like we had done something wrong. Even I, was dead sure that we had come back out exactly the way we had gone in, and yet there was no deer. I remember my uncle saying, "Am I out of my mind? Where's the damn buck?"

It took all of about twenty seconds for my dad to look down and see some drag marks, which took his eyes directly to what was the pole tree laying just up the path with the ropes beside it. As we walked over to it, my uncle reached down and picked up the ropes and said, "These damn things were snapped." My dad grabbed one and agreed, "You're right. These weren't cut. They were broken off." My uncle cursed angrily, "Son of a bitch, all they had to do was untie the damn knot if you didn't want the pole." It was then that my dad said, "Hey, check this out. Look at these damn prints."

As we looked down, there were a number of very large, human-like footprints in some of the softer soil on the trail. It was then that my uncle said, "Son of a bitch! We've been ripped off by a shit-ass Booger." I had no idea what he was talking about or what a *Booger* was, but my dad was shaking his head in agreement. My uncle started shouting, "Some shit-ass, son of a bitchin' Booger followed us out and ripped off our damn deer. If that don't take the damn cake, I don't know what does. Son of a bitch, I am fighting mad!" He was crazy mad and his face showed it, while my dad just stood there rather calmly.

"Well," my dad said, "There's no sense in hanging around here and crying all day. Let's get the heck out of here." Just as we were leaving, my uncle handed me a piece of the rope and said, "You keep this, son, as a Booger souvenir." With that, he shoved the other piece in his jacket pocket. As we were walking out, with my uncle yelling and screaming, I kept looking at the rope and was trying to pull it apart myself. It was impossible. It was a half inch thick and the knots were still tied tightly. The fibers were completely torn apart from each other. I couldn't imagine what this *Booger thing* was that had the power to do this.

For the entire ride home, my uncle was shouting and pounding on the dash board, screaming that a dumbass Booger had gotten the better of two grown men. When we got home, my mother and aunt were waiting for our arrival. Before my uncle even stopped the car, he was shouting out the window how the Booger stole our deer. My mother pulled me aside and brought me into the house to wash up and have something to drink. Five minutes later, everyone was at the table while my aunt and mother were making some bacon and eggs. It was then, while we were eating breakfast, that I finally spoke up and asked if someone could tell me what a Booger is. My uncle said that it was a big, hairy-ass critter that lives in the woods and howls like a wolf.

As soon as he said that, my aunt shushed him, saying, "Don't tell him that. He'll be afraid to go outside." My dad broke in saying, "The boy is old enough to know now, especially after what happened today. The truth is always the best in all circumstances."

My dad went on to talk about this creature called, "The Hairy Man of the Woods," which some people call a Booger or a Wild Man. He said that they were known around these parts for as long as there have been people living here. They steal critters and food and kill livestock. He even said that some say they have taken people. The picture I had sent to you via email was the piece of rope that my uncle handed me in the woods that day. Until my dying day, I will never forget that day in the Tennessee woods.

The Bridalveil Falls Trail Sighting

This sighting was told to me by Valerie Romano, who was hiking through Yosemite with her girlfriend, Carol. Here is what Valerie had to say:

The craziest thing about this sighting was the location in which it had occurred. Considering all the areas in Yosemite that one would consider desolate and lightly travelled, the Bridalveil Trail would not be one of them. This particular trail is predominantly hard pack with very little elevation change or anything else for that matter. There are a decent amount of rock climbers in the area and a fair amount of foot traffic from all kinds of people who want to see the falls. In fact, a lot of single chicks come here in hopes of increasing their chances of marriage, according to the Indian legend. At any rate, Carol and I were relatively alone this day in May of 2007, when we were working our way down the trail.

The two of us have been on this trail numerous times, as we have on many of the trails in Yosemite. We were coming up on an area where there is a creek that is strewn so heavily with boulders, that it's hard to even say it's a creek. As we were approaching, we heard the sound of a large rock cracking down on top of some other rocks. There was no question in our minds whatsoever as to what we had heard and we knew it was coming from the creek. I don't think it was but fifteen seconds later that we heard yet another sound of boulders tumbling against each other, like we had the first time.

The two of us were very unsure as to what we were about to walk up on, and began to slow our roll; gradually coming up to where the sound was emanating from. As we were closing in on the creek, we heard yet another large cracking sound of a boulder tumbling. Now, this really had our attention because the boulders in this creek are more than likely in the fifty pound plus range. Some of them are probably over a hundred pounds or more. This is a boulder field with water running through it. Who or what was tossing boulders around was anyone's guess at this point. We crept up to the point where we could now turn our heads to the right, viewing the creek.

There are a lot of low lying trees in here of quite a few varieties. The creek has some trees growing up right through the boulders and is enveloped somewhat like a tunnel by trees on both sides. In the direction we were looking, the creek and boulder field meandered into the trees about seventy five feet away from where we were crouched. It was at almost the apex of where the creek disappeared to the left, into the trees, that we saw a Sasquatch.

The creature was standing directly under an area of the canopy where the sun was shining brightly on its back. It was standing on an angle, where we were seeing its back and left arm, in a hunched over position. It was holding what appeared to be a very heavy rock like it was nothing. It then flipped this boulder to its side and kind of knelt down, reaching into the water with its hand. It seemed to be feeling around in the creek and then, it put its hand to its mouth. Thankfully, it wasn't facing towards us, for only a few moments later, it took a step and picked up another boulder, flipped it to the side, and bent down to reach into the creek again.

This time, it used its left hand, which we could see, and put it to its mouth. The creature was about a hundred feet away from us, but because of the size of its hands and the smallness of whatever it was grabbing, we couldn't see anything. Mind you, I couldn't believe that the two of us had even stayed there for this amount of time and not run away.

It was just a few seconds later, that we heard some people talking and laughing, coming up the trail from where we had. As soon as we heard the noise, the Sasquatch turned its head quickly to its right, which again, was not looking at all at us, and took a couple of quick steps into the trees and was gone.

About two minutes later, these three dudes came walking up on us and said, "How are you girls doing today?" Carol said to them, "You dudes just scared off a Bigfoot." They were like, "No way man, are you kidding me?" Then Carol said, "Way, bro. He was standing right up there, flipping boulders around, and eating something. As soon as you dudes started laughing back there, he heard you and split."

The one dude said, "I am so sorry, man. Where was he?" I told him, "Don't be sorry because we were more than likely ten seconds away from running out of here. You actually did us a favor." Then one of these guys walked up to where the Sasquatch had been. He was trying his best not to break his neck on the rocks. When we watched this dude trying to make his way back to where the Sasquatch was, and how hard it was, it made me realize how easily the Sasquatch had done it.

It was no chore at all for him to move around on these boulders. This dude tried to pick up some of the rocks and we thought he would drop a nut in the process. The Bigfoot was picking them up and holding them while he was looking around in the water. Just after that, this guy said that there was a big footprint right next to the creek where he was standing. Eventually, he made his way back over by us and they left. This thing was about eight or nine feet tall, from what we could guess, and it was picking up these huge rocks like it was holding a football. It looked like there was no effort or strain whatsoever on its body. The hair in the direct sunlight was reddish blonde and the blonde could have very well been white or even grey. The sun was so bright on its back that it was actually creating a glare.

It was really a hard thing to take in as we watched. I was kind of in a stupor, like I was waiting to wake up from a dream. It's very hard to explain, but that's the way it was. For the time that we were there watching, it I felt like I was in a trance. I say that because I can't even believe that the two of us were able to just sit there and not run. I have no idea how this type of thing can even be in this area and stay out of sight. It's not like we were in some big dark rainforest and yet, there it was.

Yes, my dear readers, and yet there it was...and still is, I might add.

The Chattahoochee River Sighting

This sighting was brought to my attention by a woman named Gladys Furman, a resident of the great state of Georgia. Here is what Gladys saw in the summer of 1992:

My husband is long since passed, but at the time, the two of us were taking a canoe trip down the Chattahoochee for the day. We had begun the journey in the morning from the Jones Bridge, with our end goal being the Chattahoochee River Park. Depending on the river level and how much paddling that you want to do or not, this trip, which we have done before, can take somewhere between nine and twelve hours. The time was about 5:30 in the morning. We were about two hours into the float when we began to slowly drift around a bend in the river. On the bank to our left, my husband and I saw a large blue heron taking a fish from the shallows and swallowing it whole. The two of us put our binoculars to our eyes in order to watch the bird.

We had our eyes fixed on this bird for probably about two minutes as the canoe continued its drift in the current. When I finally had taken my glasses down and looked ahead down the river, no sooner had I turned my head then my eyes became fixed on what appeared to be two figures standing on a shoal on the river's edge. At that moment, I didn't realize that I was looking at one small creature and the larger being bent over at the waist. Both of them had their backs turned to us in the canoe. My husband still had his binoculars fixed on the heron, when I whispered to him to look.

The current was pulling us along at a pretty good clip that morning and we were gaining on where these creatures were standing fairly rapidly. When I first saw them, we were more than likely two hundred yards away and closing. When the larger one straightened up, and I now knew it was large, it twisted its upper torso to the left. I realized later that I was looking at a breast on its chest, which I didn't fully comprehend at that moment. When she had turned to the left, she must have caught a glimpse of us in her peripheral vision because, what had initially started out as a very casual movement, suddenly turned very fast as she fully turned to look at us. This larger creature, which we both realized later was a Bigfoot, reached down quickly, grabbing hold of the little one and picking it up like a mother holding a small child. She then took about three or four steps and was gone from sight into the trees on the bank.

It was only maybe two minutes later when the drift had brought us right to the spot where they had been standing. We used the paddles to hold our position and take a good look at where they had been. We could now see that there was, in fact, a shallow water shoal. Through the, maybe, one foot of water, it was evident that she had been digging around in the river bottom, possibly for some fresh water crustaceans or the like, I have no idea, but the bottom was definitely disturbed in a number of areas.

As we looked into the trees, we could see nothing of the two Bigfoot, but the trees were so dense at this point, that they could have been right there hiding and we would have been unable to see them, due to the vegetation along the river's edge, being extremely thick and lush. It was after the fact that I came to the conclusion that the smaller one must have been no more than three feet tall or so. At that height, he didn't reach the level of the mother's waist when she was bent fully downward. It was at least a foot or more shy of that level.

When the mother had stood up and fully turned to see us, it was then that I had a good look at both of the breasts and knew that it was a female and its babe. The mother was easily well over twice the height of the little one, making her some seven to eight feet tall. The mother's body was large and yet very cylindrical in its shape. From the width of its thighs to the width of the upper chest, I would have to say that it was about three feet wide, and as I say, very uniform in its dimensions.

The youngster's hair was almost black in its coloration, whereas the mother was more of an auburn or reddish color. The sun being very bright, there was absolutely no variation or guessing involved as to what exactly we were looking at. It was two Bigfoot: one great and one small. As we sat in the canoe, looking over the shoal and into the woods, I could now see that she had taken only several strides to cover almost twenty feet in order to exit the river, and that with the juvenile in her grasp. Of course now, having done much research and snooping around to learn what others have seen in regards to these creatures, I must say that this female was in no way in appearance, as those said to be like a body builder. You could evidently see that she was as powerful as a bear, if not more so, but did not give the appearance of being muscle bound by any means. She was just thickly bodied and very burly. And I am sure that she could dispatch you or me or anyone else if you messed with her cub. That's what we saw that day on the Chattahoochee River.

The Drone Footage

This account was told to me by a man who I will call Douglas Smith. He did not want his real name to be used, as he wished to remain anonymous; the reasons for which you will soon learn:

First of all, Bill, as embarrassed as I am to say so, I fall under the category of the many who, for reasons believed to be true or not, do not want my name or identity to be linked with Bigfoot. In the professional world, my opinion is that it could do me more harm than good. For that, I do apologize to you, but my family and my livelihood come first and foremost. I believe for this reason and this reason alone, thousands of people like myself have never reached out or come forward with what they have seen and or experienced in regards to this creature.

Nevertheless, I am here to share what it is that I did see, and I did see it for whatever its worth. Amongst other things, I run a professional, licensed, drone survey business. My business is involved mainly in the inspection of power transmission systems, such as power lines, wind turbines, and oil transferal systems, like our network of pipelines nationally.

Due to the nature of my business, I can find myself in some very desolate and lonely areas of North America in the course of my reporting and investigating. Without giving up any more information about my operation than I have to, the drone that I was using this day has a flight time of about twenty-five minutes, and can fly at speeds approaching fifty miles per hour. It was last year in the Midwest United States, that I was hired to do some close up photography of a string of high voltage wire towers. In years past, individual men with large cherry picker trucks had to go tower by tower to do the visual inspections that I now do with my drone.

I am typically looking to film oil leakage, bearing wear, bird nests, pipe leaks, and a host of other things that may be indicative of a team needing to come out to the location and do a formal inspection and/or repair. Generally speaking, I drive in alone as close as possible to where I am working and then, the drone takes to the air. I will typically do a fairly good inspection and then move on with my truck to close in on another area. In other words, I kind of hop scotch with my truck and the drone fills in what's in-between.

On this particular day, which was only a year ago in 2017, I was inspecting a run of power transmission poles. The section I was working on had been cut through a large swath of forest, with the terrain being somewhat like rolling hills. I had parked my Ford and began my inspection. The drone was about a mile out and going over a hill, out of my sight momentarily. When I get close to a tower, I move in tight to do a fly around, looking at all the connections for anything unusual. In between towers, I generally fly above the wires where I can get a good look at what's ahead, including the ground below. At the point which I am about to share with you, I had about twelve minutes flight time left, including about six minutes to fly the drone safely back to my location. I must add that this drone is so quiet that I could hover above you on your picnic table and you would have no idea that it was there above you.

I was on my way to the next pole, flying above the lines at about 300 feet, when my ground camera picks up on a huge Bigfoot walking along the trail which the lines are constructed on. I couldn't believe my eyes. I dropped in altitude to about 150 feet and had an incredible bird's eye view of this thing as it was walking along. I had only been following it for a few minutes when I had to bring the drone back.

As soon as the drone was secured, I jumped in the truck and took off up to the point where the drone had gone over the hill out of my sight. I parked just below the crest of the hill and relaunched my drone with a fresh battery pack in hopes of catching the Bigfoot further down the trail. Just a few minutes later, there he was. I couldn't believe how much ground he had covered since I had last seen him. True to form, this creature had no idea that it was being surveilled from above. At one point, I shifted the drone to maybe fifty feet left of the Bigfoot, but at a higher altitude. I didn't want to risk for one split second that he would see the drone and for whatever reason get spooked. I could also see from the air that he was leaving numerous tracks in some of the softer areas of sand and soil on the trail.

The creature was massive and from above, it looked like the comic book character, The Hulk. It was a muscle bound monster in every sense of the word. The upper body, including its arms and torso, were pumping along as though it had so much muscle it couldn't relax its posture. Picture Mr. Universe times five; that's what I was seeing. Its head was plugged into the very level of its shoulders. On two or three occasions, I observed it looking slightly to its left or right and the entire upper body moved to do so for the most part. It appeared that the creature did not possess the same mobility that we as humans do. Whether or not they are all like this is anyone's guess. All that I know is what I saw this one doing.

Sadly, once again, the clock was working against me and I had to cut my surveillance short, bringing the drone back to the truck and the sighting was over. As soon as I had the drone back and safely, I hopped into the truck and went over the hill. The creature was miles away from me at this point and according to my estimation, this Bigfoot had walked casually somewhere between one and a half to two miles in a little over ten minutes. I knew this to be true once the drone was back on top of it the second time.

When I got over the hill, I was riding with the window open and looking at the ground for tracks which I came upon very quickly. Now I am five foot ten and I had no idea what my stride was at the time, but it took almost three excessively long and exaggerated steps of my own to equal one of the Bigfoot's. The other thing that was immediately evident was that all of its steps were in single file. In other words, one foot placed directly in front of the other, over and over again.

The Bigfoot's body was covered in predominantly thick hair, not fur. For the most part it appeared like longer hair on the head of a man or woman, maybe between four and ten inches long, depending on what part of its body that we are talking about. Its face from the side, as well as its hands, were almost entirely black, or an extremely dark shade of grey. Its feet also had overlapping hair hanging off the sides.

I understand now, more than ever, the gut wrenching feeling of knowing that this thing is real and having no outlet to talk about it. That is to say without fear of ridicule relating to what I have seen. As a professional and having worked very hard throughout my life, I simply can't risk having the wrong person say the wrong things about me. It may leave me on the outside looking in, with regards to my work and my life and so I say nothing. It is my opinion now that these things have been known about for a long time. Especially in our day and age with the advanced night vision optics being used militarily on the ground and in the air. That and all of the tactical infrared. There is no way these things are not being picked up on and seen on a regular basis. That's my opinion and I voice it as such.

The Balloonists' Encounter

It was a deliberate act on my behalf in the placing of this account directly after the previous one. Both of the sightings having taken place from an aerial platform, so to speak. Here is what the birthday boy, Curtis Delfino, had to share about his sighting:

As I told you, Bill, this sighting occurred under the most unusual of circumstances imaginable in my opinion. It was in July of 2005 that my wife had surprised me with a balloon ride as part of my birthday gift. I wasn't quite sure how I felt about it, when I opened the envelope and saw what it was, but what else was I going to say except, "Thanks." I should tell you that I and heights don't go together so well, which is something that my new bride was not exactly aware of at the time.

For three weeks, I was biting my nails as I waited for the day of the ride to arrive. It was a Tuesday morning that we had made our way over to a large field in the countryside where the balloonist team was waiting for us. The balloon was massive in its dimensions and I have to tell you that standing alongside of it was actually quite impressive. The owner/operator, whose name was Bob, told us that its panels consisted of every color in the rainbow and my God, it was spectacular. The day was somewhat cloudy, but Bob told us that the conditions were perfect as far as flying a balloon goes. While my wife was chatting it up with one of the ground crew, I stepped aside and asked Bob if it would be alright to limit our height as we flew. He just laughed and said, "When we are at a good level for you, just give me a wink and I will know what you mean."

So my wife and I, and four other people whom we had just met, climbed into the gondola as the ropes were let go and we began our flight. After about the first fifteen minutes or so, I was beginning to calm down a little, trying to do some deep breathing without letting anyone else know I was doing so. This was actually quite funny in that about twenty minutes later, I was helping to calm down a woman who was herself getting a little anxious. We were going over many farm fields that were bordered by woodlands and after a while, we approached an area that was mostly woods. The pilot, Bob, had been holding the balloon at about 500 feet in altitude for my sake, and nobody had complained or said anything about it whatsoever. I was actually starting to enjoy myself.

As we now found ourselves going over what Bob said was a hill, he said that he was going to have a little fun and bring us down to treetop level. The balloon was actually kind of neat to see in operation. I think there were flaps that could let hot air out allowing it to descend and then, of course, when he wanted to gain altitude, he just turned the burner on to create more hot air within the balloon.

We had descended to a level where we were just barely skimming over the tops of the trees and then suddenly, we brushed them and everyone in the balloon started to cheer and laugh. We were making such a racket that you would think we had won the lottery, but it was all in good fun. Bob then allowed the balloon to gain a little more altitude and then, once again, he allowed the balloon to descend back down to treetop level. At this point, we were almost to the edge of the hill's bottom, which was also close to where this tract of woods ended. Now where this woods ended abutted with what I will call either a wheat field or a field that was resting in-between crops with something tall growing in it.

Bob once again lowered the balloon, scraping the trees, and we all erupted once again in cheers and laughter. Suddenly, one of the ladies said, "Oh my God, will you look at that!"

I was actually looking at what she saw when she said what she did. At this point we were only maybe seventy or eighty feet off the ground, having just brushed the trees, and we couldn't have had a better viewpoint. A tremendous Bigfoot had come bursting out of the forests perimeter, apparently having been frightened by the balloon hitting the trees and our screaming. He had come out into the field in a very fast walk, which would have been running for you and me. He was moving at an angle toward our right hand side and we had no way of steering the balloon to follow him.

As the creature was walking, he turned to look at us up and over his left hand shoulder. Then, he hit the ground galloping away on all fours, like a greyhound in a race! The only time I ever saw an animal move anything like that was at the Belmont Stakes horse race. In my opinion, he was actually faster than a horse. The sad thing was that he had run across the field into a narrow band of trees that was bordering it. Eventually, he would have come out and exposed himself again. However, since we were drifting in a balloon, we would not be there to see him. One of the ladies in the balloon said she thought she got a good photograph of it running away. She actually forwarded it to my wife at a later date and quite frankly, it wasn't very good at all.

That actually brings up another funny point relative to Bigfoot sightings. Everybody in that gondola had a camera, and in the heat and excitement of the moment, only one woman squeezed off a shot, and that was too late. I can tell you this much from experience having been through this now myself. The utter shock and excitement when something like this occurs is beyond description. I would compare it to awaking from a nightmare when, for a few moments, you are just trying to clear your mind and gather your thoughts. This was the same in that you momentarily can't think straight, and you temporarily lose your decision making abilities.

At any rate, when this creature came out of the woods it was just to the right-hand side of where I had been looking. I only had to shift my eyes and I was looking directly at it. It was huge and bulky. I could see its muscles moving below the fur. You know how a weight-lifter can flex their pectorals and make them kind of dance around, for lack of a better word? With every movement that this creature made, its muscles were just banging around in its body. It was really remarkable to see firsthand. As it turned its head over its shoulder to look at the balloon briefly before dropping to all fours, I actually believe it looked right at me. I could see that its face was dark grey with black lines in it.

Its fur was just slightly darker than, say, a blonde grizzly bear, if you've ever seen one. It had relatively long and straight hair that almost, as crazy as it sounds, looked like it was brushed. It appeared to be fairly clean and actually all things considered, quite a beautiful thing to behold. As you could imagine, nobody cared about what the balloon was doing or not doing anymore. We were absolutely giddy about what we had just collectively seen. To date, this is the absolute craziest thing that has ever happened to me in my life and I thought I would share it with you.

This House is Not Your Home

This evidential account was brought to my attention by Lyle Remsenberg and his wife, Tracy. Here is what the couple had to say:

My wife and I had been living in the Portland, Maine area for about ten years, when a piece of property with a nice home on it was brought to our attention by a mutual friend. This home was located a considerable distance to our north in the area of Moosehead Lake, which is one of the most beautiful regions of the state. After having gone and inspected the property, the two of us had decided to make the move. This was a beautiful, older home that was only a short ride away from the southern portion of the lake, near Greenville. Now, my wife and I are big into the gardening scene, so we spend a fair amount of our time out and about in the yard. We typically have many tools and such leaning against the shed and laying here and there around the property.

It was about the middle of the summer when the two of us had gotten sick of telling each other that we had misplaced something. We were constantly blaming each other whenever a tool could not be found. We decided to gather everything together, as far as our yard tools were concerned, and do an accounting of our inventory. After counting the tools, we determined that we were missing a four pronged rake, two spades, loping shears, and three small hand shovels. Now trust me when I tell you, that there was nobody visibly around us or our yard at any time of the day or night, unless they had snuck in unaware. When we realized that neither of us was to blame, the question now arose as to exactly who was?

It was then that my wife and I decided to call the police and file a report about the stolen property, as well as the possibility of a prowler of some sort being around. An officer showed up a short while later and took our report. All of us were in agreement, as we looked around the property, that we were in a fairly secluded area and that it would seem like a very odd thing for a thief to come in here, periodically, to steal one garden tool at a time. At any rate, the officer filed the report and told us to keep in touch if there was any further activity, in regards to theft.

I guess this would be a good time to tell you that we were right in the thick of things, as far as the forest goes. Our property consisted of a cleared five acre lot that was virtually surrounded on all sides, with the exception of the driveway, by thick Maine forest. I will also mention that our driveway was about 600 feet long and connected directly to a main road. After replacing most of the stolen tools with new ones, we had decided to keep all of the tools in the shed, with the exception of two small, garden shovels that were used more regularly. These two small, hand-held shovels were left lying on a marble topped bistro style, pedestaled table on our patio; a table that we regularly used for potting plants and other such things.

It was about two weeks after the officer had come to take report of our missing items that my wife came in from the backyard and said that both of the shovels were gone. The two of us went outside and were basically standing there scratching our heads as to what was going on with these tools. For whatever reason, we started to take a walk into the woods in the hopes of finding, or seeing, some type of clues regarding these tools. We must have been walking around for about an hour when my wife said, "Hey, check this out! There's the long handled spade."

As sure as my name is Lyle, there was our spade leaning against a tree in the woods. Not that we needed any confirmation, but all of our long handled tools had a red band of paint that we had applied to the handles. It didn't end there and, in fact, things got a little weirder. As we continued our walk, my wife once again said, "Oh my God, Lyle, look at that!" She was pointing up on an angle at a tree just ahead of us and there it was.

One of our small, potting shovels was stuck in the side of a tree about nine feet off the ground. It appeared to be buried into the trunk several inches. Now, this little shovel was made of one piece of billet aluminum that had a black rubber handle on it for comfort. Just so you understand, the edges on these are not sharp at all. In fact, they are rather blunt, maybe being about 1/16 to 1/8 of an inch thick and having a slight curvature to the business end of the tool and yet, this tool was stuck into the tree several inches and high above our heads.

My wife and I walked all the way back to the house to retrieve a six foot step ladder, as well as our camera, and walked back out to where the shovel was stuck in the tree. I opened the ladder up next to the tree and, as my wife held it, I climbed up and tried to remove the shovel. Now, this tree was a large oak and I could now see, being right on top of it, that the shovel was in a good three inches. I couldn't budge it so much as making it move in the slightest. We took a picture of it and, having made our way back home, we once again called the police. I should also tell you that we left the ladder in place by the tree so the policeman could see for himself what we were talking about.

The time frame here is critical so let me spell it out for you. It took us ten minutes to get back to the house and it was about another hour before the officer arrived. We talked at the house for about ten minutes and then it took us all about another ten or fifteen minutes to get back out to where the shovel was in the tree. So, the total time that we had been gone was about an hour and a half. As we were now nearing where we were sure we had been, my wife and I were looking of course, for the folding, six foot step ladder; the ladder that we had left set up alongside of the tree. We were more than perplexed in that we couldn't find it. Now, there was nothing unusual about the tree which the shovel was stuck into, in fact, there were hundreds of this same type of tree around.

We seemed to be walking in circles when my wife, with her eagle eyes, yet again spied out the shovel stuck in the tree, yet the ladder was nowhere to be found. You can just imagine the facial expressions of this policeman as the three of us are now standing in the woods, looking at this shovel stuck nine feet above our heads in a tree, and coupled with us saying that the ladder which we left set up for him was now missing also. He stood under the tree, shaking his head as to who or what could shove a garden shovel in to a tree like that.

He also took note of the fact that the handles end had not been beaten with anything, such as a hammer. He now fully believed us about the missing ladder. We were all looking around for any type of clues on the ground and could find nothing, so back to the house we went.

The policeman said that he was going to turn this over to their detective unit for further investigation, which he did. The very next morning, my wife was outside amending some of the vegetable garden's soil with some manure. In case you're not a gardener, the whole manure thing can make your yard a little stinky for a few days, and our yard was in fact stinky.

That afternoon, the detective came by and we walked him back into the woods to see the shovel. As he stood there, he was as baffled as the three of us had been the day before, as to how the shovel could come to be where it was, and why all of our tools had gone missing. Lyle and I knew that there was nothing they could really do, shy of catching someone red handed. The detective left, having made the usual run of the mill comments regarding the incident.

It was two days later that my wife had gone out into the backyard to tend to the garden in her usual way. The garden that she had freshly manured was penned in with six foot tall chicken wire and measured fifteen by twenty-five feet. This garden was comprised of half tomatoes and half lettuce and the tomatoes were on the vine, so to speak. On one corner, there was a gate made of two by fours with chicken wire stapled to them. The gate had a simple stockade fence type of clasp on it with no lock. The supports for the wire surrounding the garden, with the exception of where the gate was built, were the long, flat, metal stakes used to support snow fencing. These were driven into the ground with a mallet type of device and afterwards, we wired the fencing to them.

A few minutes after she had gone out of the back door, she came bursting back into the house telling me, "Honey, you have to come out here and take a look at this."

We went out the door to find a section of the chicken wire was collapsed to the ground and the gate was still closed. We stood there looking at the damage and our eyes were immediately drawn to what was a large amount of huge footprints within the garden's soil. Looking at the plants, the tomatoes had been ransacked. There wasn't a single tomato left on the vines, be they green or ripened. The prints were enormous and had virtually flattened the majority of the bed. Almost every head of lettuce that had been growing was smashed.

I had gone into the house to retrieve a tape measure. The footprints measured some twenty inches long and, at the widest point, being the toes, eleven inches. They were in the shape of gigantic, human-like feet. We immediately called the detective who had left us his card, and he showed up some two hours later. When he entered the yard and saw for himself what we had described on the phone, he was momentarily speechless. When he broke the silence, he said, "I believe these are the footprints of a Bigfoot, as crazy as that may sound." He said that they do get reports of such creatures in the state from time to time, but never had he imagined that he would be looking down on such evidential proof.

The detective continued, "Everything makes sense now. Something with feet this large must be of enormous stature and strength. Calls have come in through the years of people claiming to have seen creatures ranging between seven and twelve feet tall, crossing the street or around their properties. This creature, be it mischievous or inquisitive, must have been grabbing your tools simply because it could, not knowing what they were. And for whatever reason, had driven the shovel into the tree. It would also explain the height at which it was done." He said that he felt bad, but that there was nothing they could really do. He apologized and said he would pass it on to the wardens.

After he had left, my wife and I sat down for a little chat. We were discussing all of the things that had transpired, including the notion that there was now a Bigfoot patrolling our property. The first thing that had drawn us to purchase this home was a very good price tag. The second was that the previous owners had created the garden beds we were now using, including the one that had the tomatoes in it. The thought came to us they had more than likely moved for the same reasons that we were now going to, and we sold the house.

We had been living in Maine for quite some time and had heard rumors here and there through the years of such creatures prowling about. One thing that needs to be understood about Maine, is that this state is as big as the rest of New England combined. Having said that, over ninety percent of the state is uninhabited wilderness where apparently everything and anything is roaming around out there, including a giant who can ram a shovel into a tree.

As a point of interest, my dear readers, I personally took my own gardening hand shovel and went out into the yard in an attempt to jab it into a tree. When I did so, I hurt my wrist and merely chipped a small piece of bark off. Be very careful as you wander around out there in the woods, for in so doing, you may be the next person who encounters Bigfoot.